I wouldn't be here, Mallory."

"Just doing my job." She shifted uncomfortably. Joe was too close.

"I wasn't talking about you *making* me live."

"Then what?"

"If not for you, I wouldn't have a *reason* to live." Joe moved closer. "I know I've made mistakes. More than a man's entitled to make in a lifetime. I won't ask you to overlook the past. But is there any way you could bring yourself to think about the future instead?"

Mallory gulped to loosen the knot in her larynx. His gentle touch had ignited a riot of emotions inside her. Longing, desire, joy and sadness, exploding in turn like a string of firecrackers. Her resistance evaporated, and she leaned toward him, pulled by a need stronger than any she'd ever known.

Mallory sighed in resignation as Joe's lips found hers. She was only human. How could she be expected to fight a force as powerful as fate?

Dear Reader,

If you're like me, you can't get enough heartwarming love stories and real-life fairy tales that end happily ever after. You'll find what you need and so much more with Silhouette Romance each month.

This month you're in for an extra treat. Bestselling author Susan Meier kicks off MARRYING THE BOSS'S DAUGHTER—the brand-new six-book series written exclusively for Silhouette Romance. In this launch title, *Love, Your Secret Admirer* (#1684), our favorite matchmaking heiress helps a naive secretary snare her boss's attention with an eye-catching makeover.

A sexy rancher discovers love and the son he never knew, when he matches wits with a beautiful teacher, in *What a Woman Should Know* (#1685) by Cara Colter. And a not-so plain Jane captures a royal heart, in *To Kiss a Sheik* (#1686) by Teresa Southwick, the second of three titles in her sultry DESERT BRIDES miniseries.

Debrah Morris brings you a love story of two lifetimes, in *When Lightning Strikes Twice* (#1687), the newest paranormal love story in the SOULMATES series. And sparks sizzle between an innocent curator—with a big secret—and the town's new lawman, in *Ransom* (#1688) by Diane Pershing. Will a seamstress's new beau still love her when he learns she is an undercover heiress? Find out in *The Bridal Chronicles* (#1689) by Lissa Manley.

Be my guest and feed your need for tender and lighthearted romance with all six of this month's great new love stories from Silhouette Romance.

Enjoy!

Mavis C. Allen
Associate Senior Editor, Silhouette Romance

Please address questions and book requests to:
Silhouette Reader Service
U.S.: 3010 Walden Ave., P.O. Box 1325, Buffalo, NY 14269
Canadian: P.O. Box 609, Fort Erie, Ont. L2A 5X3

When Lightning Strikes Twice

DEBRAH MORRIS

Soulmates

SILHOUETTE *Romance*®

Published by Silhouette Books

America's Publisher of Contemporary Romance

For my critique partner, Diana Ball,
who made a suggestion that led to an idea
that created a character that resulted in a book.
Thank you for the inspiration and
for sharing your flashlight when the journey gets dark.

 SILHOUETTE BOOKS

ISBN 0-373-19687-3

WHEN LIGHTNING STRIKES TWICE

Copyright © 2003 by Debrah Morris

Visit Silhouette at www.eHarlequin.com

Printed in U.S.A.

Books by Debrah Morris

Silhouette Romance

A Girl, a Guy and a Lullaby #1549
That Maddening Man #1597
Tutoring Tucker #1670
When Lightning Strikes Twice #1687

DEBRAH MORRIS

Before embarking on a solo writing career, Debrah Morris coauthored over twenty romance novels as one half of the Pepper Adams/Joanna Jordan writing team. She has changed careers several times in her life, but much prefers writing to working.

Readers may contact her via her Web site: www.debrahmorris.com.

INTEROFFICE MEMO

To: Celestian, Heavenly Air Traffic Controller

From: A Texas Ranger Destined To Reunite with His Soulmate

Date: Right Now

Re: Simple Request

Dear C—

Given that I'm a straggler up here on a fluffy cloud, I'd *really* like to return to earth and somehow occupy a body so that I can be reunited with my love, Dr. Mallory Peterson. I mean, I'm not really doing anything up here. As a Texas Ranger, I see my work isn't needed in heaven.

So, whaddya say?

Eternally,
A Man in Love

Prologue

"Send me to heaven, or send me to hell. Just get me out of here!"

"Keep your voice down." As time-out monitor, Celestian had to maintain his composure at all times, but even a saint's serenity wasn't safe around Will Pendleton's troublesome spirit. Without ever making it past Reception, he had managed to get himself deemed Unfit for Return and to get Celestian busted down to a position devoid of prestige.

"I had no idea being dead could be so danged boring." The restless soul paced the confines of the holding area.

"You're here to learn acceptance, and you're stuck until you do."

"All right, then. I accept. I'm ready to move on. I'll do whatever it takes. Now get me out of this nowhere place. Molly has been reborn, and I miss her." Despair tempered his belligerence. "I gotta know. Will I ever return to her?"

"In time." Celestian felt sorry for Pendleton, even if he was a pain in the astral. No one liked to see soul mates separated.

"I ain't got a lot of time, bub. If I was to go back now, I'd have to start out as a baby. What kind of fool plan is that?"

"One that works just fine for us, thank you."

"But Molly's already grown. I don't want her pinning my drawers.

"Time is irrelevant."

"Maybe here in limbo land. But dang it, I've been cooling my heels in this milky joint for a hundred years. A hundred years today!"

"Happy anniversary. Please take your seat." Had it only been a century? Seemed longer. Time didn't fly when you weren't having fun.

"No! I ain't taking my seat. I've been sitting for a century. I need wrongs to right and laws to serve. I should be on earth catching crooks and protecting the innocent, not here jawing with a yahoo like you."

Celestian rolled his eyes. Just because Pendleton's destiny was to stand up for truth, justice and honor, didn't mean he had to be so self-righteous about it.

Due to his untimely end as a Texas Ranger, the warrior spirit had yet to complete his cosmic cycle. He had evolved through many lifetimes, serving variously as village constable, musketeer, palace guard, crusading knight and tribal warrior, but as Will Pendleton, he had arrived too soon, leaving unfinished business on earth.

The Ranger leaned across the desk, invading space that was not his. "I feel useless. Give me something to do." His conversational style hadn't improved much. He'd arrived making demands and was still doing so ten decades later. "I ain't used to living in a sitting position."

Celestian smiled. "Technically, you're no longer living at all."

An angry, insubstantial fist slammed onto the desk without disturbing the tranquility of the white, soundless room. "I'm dead because you made a mistake, you pea-brained fool."

"You are not dead," Celestian corrected. "You are currently not living."

He snorted. "Pardon the hell outta me if I can't appreciate the difference."

"You are not living because you slipped your mortal coil. You know that."

"I *know* all right. I know my *mortal coil* got a decent burial back in Slapdown in 1903. I know the whole town mourned my passing, and some of my *compadres* even sobbed at my graveside. I know the woman I was meant to spend my life with died a sad and lonely old spinster because you yanked me back before my time. That's what I *know*."

"Spirits live forever. Mortal coils decline and die. Maybe you weren't listening the first ten thousand times I explained the transmutation process." Celestian concealed his irritation. The Boss frowned on displays of human emotions. Conversations between routing reps and detainees were often recorded and assessed for quality assurance.

Backsliding was duly noted during evolvement reviews. Since being demoted to time-out monitor, Celestian had been cited more than once for acting too human. It wasn't his fault. Pendleton could provoke a senior-level saint.

The situation had begun innocently enough. Less than a day after Celestian began working in the Department of Natural Forces, Pendleton had alighted in Reception yelling about how he'd been hot on the earthbound trail of a cold-blooded killer. Just when he had the miscreant in his sights, a lightning bolt had arrowed out of a cloudless sky and ended his life.

That assessment was a bit off. It was actually the desperado who had gotten the drop on the lawman. An Emergency Order to Intercede had been fired down to the department, and Celestian had dispatched a spear of lightning on the Ranger's behalf. New to the job, he'd miscalculated both the trajectory and heaven to earth time differential.

Misfiring lightning bolts was bad enough, but Celestian's real mistake had been admitting his error. News that the shocking end had been intended for the bad man only fired Pendleton's anger. Seems he'd been snatched from the arms of his true love three days before their wedding.

In the end, failure to accept his unscheduled death had earned him a U.F.R. designation and a trip to the cooler.

Bungling his very first assignment had earned Celestian a demotion.

"I want to go back." Pendleton paced like a caged beast. "There must be a way for me and Molly to be together." He slammed his fist into his palm, and the silence only increased his frustration. "Didn't you mention once that there's an alternate way to return?"

"If the opportunity arose, I suppose you *could* go back as a walk-in." Celestian heaved a sigh he hoped wasn't too human. "But transmutation is beyond my abilities. I'm not certified in the latest technology."

The Ranger wheeled around. "A walk-in? What's that?"

"Sometimes when a mortal coil expires, and the resident spirit alights, another can assume the body and live out its natural life. *If* the M.C. is revived in time. It's a simple transference procedure but only used in emergencies."

"I want to do it. Send me back. Now!"

Celestian scoffed. "It's not *that* simple. First, we need an appropriate M.C. You don't want to return to your beloved as a cockroach do you?"

"No. But there *is* a way we can be together? So we can live as we were meant to do before you made a hash of everything?"

He sounded so sad, so hopeful that Celestian couldn't tell him the odds against such a transfer. Pendleton's soul mate was currently living her last earthly life during which she would fulfill her destiny. At demise, her spirit would retire. She and the Ranger, lovers in many lifetimes, would spend eternity apart. An injustice that might have broken Celestian's heart, if he still had one to break.

"There *may* be a way. But it's a long shot. Transference only works if an appropriate coil becomes available at the right moment in the precise geographical location. The resident spirit must alight before the coil is revived. The chances of that happening are—"

"What? A million to one?" There he went again, being hopeful.

"At least. The paperwork's a killer. It has to be completed in triplicate and approved—"

"I'm willing to do anything, be anybody, for the chance to go back."

Celestian reluctantly keyed in the routing request. Fat chance, but miracles *had* been known to happen. A miracle was exactly what the lovesick Ranger needed.

No point telling him the real odds. That he had about as much chance of returning to his true love in her lifetime as he had of being struck by lightning.

Again.

Chapter One

A whopper of a west Texas thunderstorm was headed her way.

The hair on the back of Dr. Mallory Peterson's neck prickled the instant she stepped out the back door of the Western Plains Medical Clinic. The severe weather front, predicted to move in at midnight, had arrived ahead of schedule. Heavy black clouds boiled across the sky, and the sharp scent of rain tingled in her nostrils. She squinted in the unnatural gloom of an unseasonably hot and humid early May evening. No doubt about it. Trouble was brewing.

A stiff wind yanked the heavy door from her hands and slammed it shut with a bang. Blue-white lightning flickered on the horizon, followed by the rumble of distant thunder. She shivered, unsure whether the chill was due to dropping temperatures or a premonition of disaster.

After ten on-her-feet hours caring for a steady stream of patients, she was ready for a quiet Friday night alone with a good book and a bag of microwave popcorn. A big bag. With extra butter. She'd earned a treat. Not just for today, but also for every grueling shift she'd worked since accepting the position last autumn.

Clutching her medical bag, Mallory locked the deadbolt. If she got a move on, she could make it up the hill before the rain hit. Free living quarters close to the clinic was one of the perks of being the only physician in Slapdown. A native Texan who'd cut her teeth on cyclones, she had no qualms about riding out a little bad weather in a double-wide.

Yet, she couldn't shake the feeling that all hell was about to break loose.

She glanced over the fence dividing the parking lot from the property next door. She'd slaved all spring to keep her lawn and flower beds alive in the unseasonable heat. By what freak of horticultural nature did her neighbor's straggling patch of monster grass and gargantuan weeds grow so abundantly?

Neighbor? Squatter was more like it. The insolent, ill-mannered oaf did not pay his too-kind landlord a dollar's worth of rent. How many times had she told Brindon Tucker that helping a lazy down-and-out bum like Joe Mitchum exceeded the limits of human generosity? Unfortunately, her longtime friend was a big-hearted guy who looked for the best in people.

What he saw in Mitchum was beyond her. Texas was filled with good ole boys, but Joe wasn't one of them. After being thrown out of his manufactured home by a woman smart enough to finally divorce him, the shiftless ne'er-do-well had moved into a ratty, forty-year-old travel trailer he'd rescued from the salvage yard. Mere moments before it was scheduled to be flattened into a cube the size of a 29-inch television from the looks of it.

Aside from a few female tavern dwellers whose judgment was obviously impaired by frequent applications of hair bleach, his only regular companions were a pack of mangy dogs. None of which had ever had a bath, received a rabies vaccination or seen the inside of a vet's office.

Which only proved the adage, "No man ever sinks so low that a dog or a woman won't take up with him."

Pumped up by righteous indignation, Mallory ignored the approaching storm and her unsettling undercurrent of misgiving. She glared at the rusting car bodies and heaps of scrap metal. How had Mitchum managed to accumulate such an impressive collection of junk in the few short months he'd lived there? The place was a scandal and a danger to community health. It was a veritable wonderland of tetanus just waiting for an unsuspecting victim to stumble and puncture something. She shuddered at the thought of the chiggers, toxic ticks and poisonous snakes lurking in the overgrown brush.

She'd lodged numerous official complaints about the eyesore on the clinic's behalf. The citizens of Slapdown subscribed to a "live and let live" policy, but that hadn't stopped her from trying to convince the town council to issue a citation. Warnings hadn't worked. Maybe if they made it official and ordered Mitchum to clean up the place, haul off his junk and mow the offending vegetation, things would change.

Oh, wait. Something *had* changed. Another gutted auto hulk had been added to the landscape. According to the mayor's wife from whose shoulder Mallory had removed a questionable mole this afternoon, the lazy redneck had laughed in response to the last warning.

"Sure thang," he'd said. "Soon's I get around to it, I'll have the place lookin' fresh and dewy as The First Lady's rose garden."

The heavy clouds squeezed out a few fat raindrops, which practically bounced off the hard, dry ground. Mallory bolted for home, jogging over the well-tended clinic grounds where flowers bloomed in color-coded symmetry and grass was not permitted to grow longer than three inches. She glanced up to track the storm, and a disturbing sight stopped her in her tracks.

Joe Mitchum was perched atop a utility pole on the clinic side of the fence. Dressed in scruffy jeans and a T-shirt, he looked grungy even from a distance. His precarious position was loosely secured by a makeshift lineman's harness. She had never mistaken him for a genius, but lightning was flashing, and the man was clinging to the highest object in an otherwise open area. Tampering with electrical wires.

Somewhere a village was missing its idiot.

The wind kicked up as she dashed across the parking lot. She stopped at the bottom of the pole and looked up. Rain stung her face like liquid needles. "Hey! What do you think you're doing up there?"

"Borrowing a little juice. Power's out." Mitchum grinned down at her. He had an annoyingly wide smile that revealed naturally straight, white teeth. Had to be natural. No way did orthodontia fit into his unemployed slacker budget. Heck, the four-syllable word wouldn't fit into his caveman vocabulary.

As far as she knew, there had been no power outages in the area. Mitchum's electricity had probably been cut off due to failure to pay. "Are you crazy? Or just plain stupid?"

"I'm a wrestling fan," he called over the wind. "Wanna come over and watch the WWF with me tonight? You can bring a six-pack."

What a waste of decent looks and bulging muscles. While he could be creepily charming at times, she'd rather break both her thumbs than set foot in his tumbledown, flea-infested trailer shack. "In case you haven't noticed, there's a storm rolling in."

"Better get inside then. You're so sweet, Doc, the rain might melt you."

A few ginger-colored curls had escaped the ponytail elastic securing her unruly mop. She pushed an errant strand of wet hair out of her eyes. "I realize Mr. Hardy flunked you out of physics class, but are you at all familiar with the basics of electrical conduction?"

"Yep. Electricity makes the world go around. Or does love do that?"

"You're hugging a lightning rod there, Einstein." Mitchum had been two grades ahead of Mallory throughout junior high and high school. She'd finished at the top of her class, earned a full college scholarship, gone on to graduate summa cum laude from Baylor Medical School.

Joe had dropped out a month before his own high school commencement for reasons known only to his unambitious self. In the twelve years since, he'd accomplished nothing noteworthy, nor done anything even remotely useful. Unless you counted his career as the poster child for brainless wonders.

Then there was his precocious three-year-old daughter, Chloe. Mallory recalled the adorable preschooler from a recent clinic visit. Mitchum's ex-wife Brandy had recently moved to a neighboring town to live with her parents but continued to bring her child to the clinic. She was doing an admirable job of raising Chloe, but the little girl deserved more than the paltry child support Joe managed to scrape together each month, and occasional court-mandated visits.

While he'd never been caught committing a crime, Mitchum had no visible means of support. He called himself a mechanic and sported the dirty fingernails to prove it, but Mallory had never met anyone whose car he had actually repaired. Judging from the automotive debris littering his yard, he was more adept at taking them apart than he was at putting them back together.

"You'd better shinny down that pole," she called up to him. Unless you have a burning desire to be a fried hick on a stick.

"Don't get your panties in a knot, Doc." He pulled the steel spike strapped to his boot out of the pole and lowered it a notch. Repeating the move with the other foot, he started down. "I'm done."

So was she. Her hair was soaked, and she was cold. If the bozo wanted to risk electrocution in order to watch half-naked overweight men throw chairs at each other, who was she to question his choice of entertainment? Joe Mitchum wasn't worth catching pneumonia, and she had a date with some hot buttery popcorn.

She turned and stalked away. Tomorrow she'd have a little chat with Nate Egan, the county sheriff. Texas hadn't passed any laws against being a dumb jerk, but bootlegging power was definitely illegal.

She was halfway across the parking lot when a bright spear of lightning knifed to earth, followed by a deafening boom of thunder. The distinctively pungent odor of ozone assaulted her nostrils, and her scalp tingled as the super-charged air lifted her hair. Heart racing, she wheeled around and gasped. Popping, crackling flames erupted from the reduction transformer atop the utility pole. A shower of sparks, like a miniature fireworks display, cascaded to the ground and rained upon the still, silent body of Joe Mitchum.

With no thought for her own safety, Mallory surged into doctor mode and rushed to the fallen man's side. Kneeling beside him, she immediately assessed his condition. Eyes closed, skin pale beneath a dark three-day growth of beard, he lay motionless as drops of rain splashed onto his face. She checked his airway and palpated his carotid for a pulse, silently willing him not to die.

His shirt and jeans were tattered, but he didn't appear to be burned. The bolt of lightning had probably not struck him directly. More likely, the current had zinged down the pole, conducting a charge through the steel spikes attached to his boots. Still, he wasn't breathing, and the electrical shock had stopped his heart.

She crouched beside him, punched 9-1-1 into the cell phone clipped to the waistband of her slacks and ordered the dispatcher to send an ambulance from the hospital in Midland. It would not arrive for at least fifteen minutes, and she couldn't afford to waste another second. Just as she initiated cardiopulmonary resuscitation, the clouds opened up, and a cold rain poured onto her and the man whose life was now in her shaking hands.

She pinched his nostrils shut and sealing her lips firmly over his, administered a series of life-giving breaths. Under normal circumstances, she never would have allowed their lips to touch, but nothing was normal now. When she determined he still wasn't breathing, she locked the fingers of her hands together and delivered the rhythmic chest compressions needed to keep his heart beating and blood flowing. An average human brain could survive only three or four minutes of oxygen deprivation, but this was no average man.

Joe Mitchum couldn't afford to lose any brain cells.

Fifteen compressions, two breaths. Mallory performed the cycle over and over. After four unbelievably long minutes, she heard him gasp in a breath. Color gradually seeped back into his face, but she still couldn't detect a pulse.

"Come on back, Mitchum." Mouth-to-mouth was no longer required, so she straddled her patient for better leverage. The change of position gave her tired arms a respite. Counting aloud, she rocked forward with each cycle of compressions. Keep breathing, you stupid son of…don't die on me. Being only human, it occurred to her that his death would be no great loss to the world. In fact, his untimely end might have been ordained by a higher power.

The thought shocked and sickened her. What was she thinking? She was a doctor who'd sworn an oath to save lives, no matter how wasted that life might be. And what about little Chloe? The child needed a father. The poor kid had the rotten luck to be stuck with a lousy one, but Joe was only thirty years old. He still had time to turn his life around and make something of himself.

If he lived.

"Come back to me, dammit." Grimly determined and focused on her task, Mallory lost track of time as the rain pelted down, soaking her cotton blouse and khaki slacks, and plastering her hair against her head. She'd never administered one-man CPR in a real life-or-death situation, and the extended effort tightened her muscles into hot knots. She sighed with relief when the shrieking ambulance siren wailed in the distance.

The unconscious man probably couldn't hear, but she spoke to him anyway. "Hold on, Joe. The paramedics are coming. If you can make it to the hospital, you have a chance. Hang in there for Chloe. Don't die."

Please, God, don't let him die. It was a plea and a prayer. She only hoped Someone was listening.

His eyes fluttered open. During his last life as a Texas Ranger, Will Pendleton had sure enough woke up in some pretty strange places. Border town bordellos. Fancy Fort Worth hotels. Gulf-front flophouses. He'd even come to at the bottom of a dry well once after a gang of drunken malfeasants had knocked him out and thrown him down the hole. Plenty of times, he'd awakened with nothing but the wide blue sky over his head and the cold ground beneath him. The best place for a man to wake up was in a sweet woman's arms, but in his line of work, he'd learned to be alone.

His skin bristled like a nervous colt's. It was one thing to wake up in a strange place. Waking up in a strange body was a whole new experience.

When his blurred vision cleared, the only thing familiar was the color of his surroundings. Everything was white. Besides his own, there were five other beds in the room. All held forms draped with white sheets and attached to contraptions that made noises like birds trying to chirp.

He lifted his head for a better look-see, but it flopped weakly onto the pillow. Two women, dressed in blue pajamas like the Chinese laundryman used to wear, tended the folks in the beds. He heard their murmuring voices, but couldn't make out what they said. Their soft, white shoes made no sound on the floor.

He tried to move, but he was hog-tied by some kind of cord that ran from a needle taped to the inside of his elbow to a bag of clear liquid suspended from a metal pole. A fancy clothes-peg attached to another cord clamped painlessly on the end of his finger. He examined the hand. Long-fingered, callused and sun-brown, it had obviously belonged to a hard-working man.

Where was he? Had the transference been completed? It was possible he hadn't returned at all, but was stuck in yet another corner of Reception, still awaiting a routing assignment. The thought that he might not have made it back to earth—back to his precious Molly—filled him with aching sadness.

He wouldn't get another chance. Celestian had barely explained the possibility of walking-in when an appropriate mortal coil had been vacated. At the right time. In the right location. He wasn't too clear on events after that. Everything had happened fast. So fast the time-out monitor had little opportunity to give instructions, issue cautions or provide historical updates. He only knew one thing for sure. Due to another stunning accident, the spirit inhabiting the mortal coil known as Joe Mitchum had alighted unexpectedly in Reception, his life over and his number up.

In her assigned role as healer, Molly, or Mallory as she was now called, had persevered until she revived the uninhabited coil. According to Celestian, the resident spirit had given up first reenter rights, electing to remain in the Reception queue in hopes of receiving a better assignment.

That's when things had gotten really lively. Celestian started squawking about how they only had a small window of opportunity during which another spirit could take over, *if* Mallory succeeded in snatching the coil back from the brink of permanent death. He hadn't been blowing smoke when he said he'd do anything, take any form, to go back. He had snatched the walk-in opening without considering the implications. Like a baseball player who had spent a hundred seasons on the bench—during which all the rules had changed—he was unexpectedly thrust back in the game.

At least he hoped that's what had happened.

Thankfully, he'd observed Molly/Mallory often enough on the spirit monitor to know some of the details of her Molly life. In 1973, at age ninety-seven, she'd passed over quietly in her sleep. She had returned as Mallory, born later the same year to a hard-working local couple. Because memories of past jaunts were mercifully deleted before reentry, Mallory recalled nothing of Molly's existence or any of the other lives she'd lived.

That was the way it had to be.

Oh, yeah. He knew something else. Celestian had emphasized this was the last chance for his warrior spirit and her healer spirit to unite. They would not share the rest of these lives, nor would they be allowed to spend eternity as mates, unless she fell in love with him this time around.

That, too, was the way it had to be.

Another half-formed memory floated into his thoughts. Celestian had yelled something just before he'd been sucked into the new coil. What was it? Thinking only made his head hurt worse, but he had to remember. Celestian had been so danged insistent, it must have been important. He closed his eyes, concentrating until the monitor's words came back to him.

Yeah. He could never tell Molly/Mallory who he really was, or reveal any details of their past lives together. It was against the rules.

That was the way it had to be.

The fact that Molly was Mallory, and he was now Joe complicated things. What if she didn't recognize him? She might not even like him. Uncertainty gnawed at him, and he calmed his fears by telling himself it shouldn't be too difficult to win Mallory's heart. Not after all they'd been through together. Not after all the lifetimes they'd shared.

When he moved, pain ricocheted through his body and settled in his sore, bandaged feet. Being cooped up in the cooler with that ornery hombre Celestian for a hundred years had been a trial. Getting a ticket home had been nothing short of a miracle. Lying still when he wanted to crawl off the bed and search for the woman who would help him fulfill his destiny by fulfilling her own? That required every shattered bit of his willpower.

He tried to relax. The hard part of this trip was behind him. Charming Dr. Mallory Peterson into falling in love with him again, even after a lifetime apart, would be simple.

As easy as eating pie.

He must have nodded off for a while, because when he awoke again one of the pajama-clad women was fussing around the machinery by his bed.

"There you are, Mr. Mitchum. You're back."

"Am I?" Dry and raw at the same time, his throat was so sore he couldn't make spit or speak above a whisper. "Am I still in Reception?"

"Oh, no, sir. You're in the ICU."

He groaned in frustrated agony. Why couldn't people call things by their proper names? "What is this place?"

"The hospital. You had an accident. Don't you remember?"

"Not much. Who are you?"

"I'm Kathy. I'll be your nurse tonight." She smiled and wrapped a heavy cloth tightly around his upper arm, squeezing a small bulb until it tightened uncomfortably. After a few seconds, she released the bulb. "Your blood pressure is almost normal. How do you feel?"

"Like I've been lightning-struck."

She patted his arm. "I'm not surprised. Take it easy now, the doctor will be in to see you soon."

"Is that Mol—er, Mallory?" The name didn't feel as strange coming out of his mouth as he thought it would. "Is she here?"

"You mean Dr. Peterson? I don't know. Would you like to see her?"

"Yes." A rush of emotion tightened his damaged throat and threatened to cut off his breathing again. "Please." He'd waited a hundred years for this moment. Mallory Peterson looked nothing like his former fiancée, midwife Molly Earnshaw. Nor did her appearance match any of the other mortal coils she'd inhabited over time. Still, he couldn't wait to see her. From tribal bonesetter to medieval herbalist to village wise woman, she'd always been a healer. Now she was a doctor. She'd finally reached the goal she'd yearned after so long.

The nurse picked up his wrist, felt his hammering pulse, frowned and wrote something on a paper clamped to a board. "I don't know if Dr. Peterson is still in the building, she may have gone home by now."

"No!" Not seeing her would hurt more than the injuries he'd suffered.

"Okay, calm down. I'll have her paged. Maybe she's still around."

"Thank you. Please, just find her."

The woman tucked the sheet around him. "You rest, and I'll see what I can do."

"I have to see her," he whispered tightly. He had to. He couldn't wait another moment.

"It was the darnest thing I ever saw." After changing into clean green surgical scrubs, Mallory sat in the doctor's lounge with a cup of coffee. She related the evening's events to Andrew "Mac" McKinley, the on-call physician who'd taken charge of Joe in the emergency room. "I'm telling you, that fork of lightning hit the pole like a heat-seeking missile. It was almost as though it had made a special trip down from heaven, specifically to strike him."

Mac shook his head. "I'm surprised at you, Mal. That's not a very scientific explanation for someone with an undergrad major in physics."

"I know, but it was still pretty amazing."

"What's amazing is the fact he's still alive. You saved his life, you know."

"I did, didn't I?" She grinned. "That's what we're here for, right? Mallory Peterson's my name, saving lives is my game."

"Are you planning to hang around until our patient wakes up?"

"I'm thinking about it." Mac was an excellent physician. She had no reservations about handing off Joe's care. Yet, she felt responsible for the man whose heart had resumed beating under her hands. She'd insisted on riding to Midland in the ambulance with him and had assisted in the initial assessment. She didn't understand, and couldn't explain to her colleague, the indefinable connection she felt for the man she'd brought back from death.

"Inconsiderate of him to get toasted on a Friday night," Mac teased. "Don't you have anything better to do?"

"No. I'll just see how he's doing before I go."

"Suit yourself."

Mallory was relieved when he didn't chide her about her absentee social life. That would have to wait, until she'd proved to the town that their faith in her had not been misplaced. Too bad time was finite. A limited resource, it ran out. Got used up. Squandered. Every life was allotted a certain number of minutes, and they were too precious to waste. She'd already spent an inordinate amount of her allotted time pursuing her dream.

She hoped she'd made the right decision. Although becoming a physician had never felt like her decision to make. For reasons neither she nor her family understood, she had wanted to be a doctor even before she knew what a doctor was. When she was two and a half, her mother claimed she had grabbed the pediatrician's stethoscope, cried, "Mine!" and refused to let go.

Her fate had been sealed when her parents had given her a toy doctor kit for her third birthday. She'd spent all her play-time clumsily bandaging imaginary injuries sustained by her dolls and dispensing invisible pills to her patients. At five, when her father bragged that she might grow up to be a nurse, she'd stamped her foot. "No," she'd declared. "I'm gonna be a doctor."

The story made an amusing family anecdote, but achieving her dream had not been easy. She came from a working-class home where money was tight and ambitions realistic. Her father drove a big rig back and forth across the country, and her mother waited tables. They knew their daughter was as smart as she was dedicated, but financing the education necessary to complete medical training seemed beyond their reach.

In typical driven fashion, Mallory had seized control of the situation. Even in junior high, she had willingly sacrificed her personal life on the altar of ambition, studying hard to make grades that would attract the attention of scholarship committees. She saved most of the money she made working at the Bag and Wag after school, weekends and summers, and still found time to volunteer and participate in extracurricular activities.

When she'd earned a scholarship to Thorndyke College, the people of Slapdown had banded together to raise money for additional expenses. Throughout her undergraduate years, and later at Baylor, they'd sent her a small monthly stipend. They said it was because they believed in her. Knowing folks who had never realized their own dreams wanted to be part of hers made all the work worthwhile.

She was lucky to have that kind of support, and she had made them a promise. When she received her medical license, she would return to her hometown and dedicate herself to caring for the people who had helped her. In its one hundred-and-twenty-year history, Slapdown had never had a full-time doctor. Now little Mallory Peterson was responsible for the health and well-being of its citizens.

She still couldn't believe it.

As a further gesture of good faith, Brindon Tucker, another local boy who'd made good, had built Western Plains Medical Clinic with money won in the state lottery. She'd come home to run the state-of-the-art facility, hanging out her shingle as soon as the ink on her license had dried.

Under her management, the number of people served by the clinic had grown since the doors opened last fall. Once word got out, residents of neighboring towns and rural areas sought care at Western Plains. The staff included a nurse practitioner, an RN, a medical assistant and an office manager. Not bad for a town that had never had its own doctor before.

Mac was refilling their coffee cups when Mallory's beeper chirped. She answered the page on the lounge phone. When she hung up, she turned to the other doctor. "Mitchum's awake."

Mac gulped down the lukewarm brew, and they hurried out into the corridor. "Did the nurse say anything?"

"Just that he asked to see me."

"I'll need to assess his cognitive function to determine whether he suffered brain damage," Mac said as the elevator doors closed.

"Well, the guy was on a utility pole stealing electricity during a storm," she reminded. "All things considered, I'm not sure you'll be able to tell."

The Ranger opened his eyes when the man with Mallory introduced himself. "I'm Dr. McKinley. I guess you know Dr. Peterson."

"Yes, sir." He'd known her so long, she seemed like an extension of his own being. She looked different, yet he knew her immediately. He would have recognized the spark in her warm sherry-colored eyes anywhere. For a hundred years, he'd longed to kiss her heart-shaped lips. "I owe you my thanks, Doc."

"It's a miracle I was there when it happened," she said.

"They don't call it a miracle," he muttered.

"What?" she asked.

"Never mind." He had to be careful. He was somebody else now. He could not reveal himself and had to start thinking like this Joe fella before anyone got suspicious. Will Pendleton, Texas Ranger, was gone, dead over a hundred years. He no longer existed, not even as a memory. Molly, the last person who might have held him in her thoughts, was long gone, too.

There was no turning back now. He'd bet it all when he did a walk-in to Joe Mitchum's life. But who was the man whose coil he now inhabited? What was he like? What kind of relationship did he have with Mallory? Blessing or curse, he didn't know much about Joe. He was on his own.

Dr. McKinley explained his medical condition, reassuring him he'd sustained no long-term physical damage. His feet were injured because the steel spikes on his boots had conducted an electrical charge through them as it exited his body. The second-degree burns were limited and would respond well to treatment. Joe was a very lucky man, given the fact that he'd just been struck by lightning.

"When can I get out of here?"

"Don't be in a hurry," McKinley said. "When you're feeling stronger, we'll run some tests. If everything checks out, you should be able to go home in a couple of days." The doctor's belt chirped, and he excused himself, explaining he had rounds to make.

"What's wrong with those folks?" He gestured to the forms in the other beds. "Did they come back, too?"

Mallory frowned. She'd watched him with a confused expression since arriving in the ICU. "What do you mean, come back?"

"Nothing. I didn't mean anything." He didn't want Mallory to leave. He'd waited so long to be with her; now that she was here, a few minutes were not enough. He wanted more. "The nurse said you saved my life."

She shrugged. "All in a day's work. Do you remember what happened?"

"Not much." He closed his eyes because they were tired and heavy. What could he tell her? That the first thing he'd become aware of as Joe Mitchum was the weight of her body as she straddled him to pound on his chest? That her warmth had comforted him? That he'd recognized her familiar scent? He'd settled uneasily into his new body, like a weary man cramming his feet into boots a size too small. Knowing she was there had made the transition easier.

He was still grappling with the knowledge that a stopped heart could be made to beat again. It was truly a wonder. One of the last things Celestian had said was how there had been all kinds of changes in the world since he'd left it last. The time-out monitor hadn't gotten a chance to explain those changes. He'd promised that although Joe's mental and emotional memories were gone, departed with his alighted spirit, Joe's physical memories would kick in once Will's spirit acclimated to the unfamiliar coil.

"Why don't you tell me what happened?" He'd say anything to keep her near a little longer.

"Not tonight. You've been through an ordeal. Don't try to talk. You need to rest." She stood uneasily by the bed, shifting from foot to foot as though torn between the desire to go, and an inexplicable urge to stay. "I'll try to stop by tomorrow to see how you're doing."

When she turned to leave, he grabbed her hand, and held it. "Don't go!" Sadly, he couldn't remember how her skin felt against his own. Yet there was something infinitely right about their touch.

She must have felt it, too. Surprise and shock washed over her face as she pulled her hand from Joe's. She stepped back and folded her arms across her chest. "Dr. McKinley is a fine physician. He'll take good care of you."

"I want you."

She blinked, as though he'd spoken in a language so foreign she could not comprehend his meaning. "What?"

He struggled to sit, but she pressed him back onto the bed. "Don't try to get up. Rest. Please."

He stared into her golden brown eyes, and for a fleeting moment, he glimpsed the healer he had loved so much. Overcome with emotion, he flung his arms around her, pulling her close in a fierce bear hug that nearly upset the pole with the hanging bag. "I want you…to be my doctor."

Tensing, she pulled from his desperate embrace to right the pole and stepped behind a shield of professionalism. Did she think it would protect her from personal involvement? She cleared her throat. "Maybe I can see you on an outpatient basis after your discharge. *If* you require additional care."

She watched him closely, but he couldn't tell if she was attracted or repelled by what she saw. Before she could be swayed by either emotion, she spun on her heels and pushed her way through the swinging door. He couldn't do or say anything to stop her.

He slumped back on the bed, longing burning in him like a fever. He could almost taste the acrid tang of disappointment on his tongue. He couldn't reveal himself, and there had been no spark of recognition in her eyes. She had no idea who he really was. When she looked at him, she saw nothing of the men he'd been, or the lives they'd shared. She saw only Joe Mitchum, a fellow unlucky enough to get himself struck by lightning.

Mallory believed he was Joe. Judging from her reaction, that fact would clearly work against him.

Chapter Two

Mallory spent Sunday afternoon cleaning house. She lived alone and was compulsively neat, so housework didn't eat up a lot of her time. She saved her least favorite chore—ritual refrigerator cleansing—for last. Trying to focus on the stimulating task of clearing out tiny dishes of petrified lasagna and mummified peas, she was distracted by Friday night's events. Leave it to Joe Mitchum to require lifesaving measures in such a bizarre and dramatic fashion.

Instead of enjoying much needed time off she had spent the weekend thinking about him and the desperate way he'd grabbed her in the hospital. The look in his eyes haunted her. He'd been glad to see her, but she'd seen more in the dark brown depths than relief. Like elation. Too bad she couldn't toss out unwanted thoughts of Joe as easily as Wednesday night's chicken.

Strangely enough, she'd felt something too. His touch had made her shiver in a wow-what's-going-on-here way. She'd had a déjà vu moment, like being hugged by Joe was nothing new. Which was absurd. She'd known Joe for years, but they'd never shared anything but animosity. Since he'd moved in next door to the clinic, he'd gone out of his way to aggravate and provoke her. So why had he been so happy to see her?

She finished spraying the inside of the fridge with antibacterial cleanser, and carefully replaced the contents on the shelves. Pickles on the left. Jelly on the right. She was imagining things. He'd been relieved to see her because...well, he'd nearly died and was probably glad to see anyone, especially the doctor who'd saved his life.

Her preoccupation with Joe was no more than professional interest. That would account for the thoughts spinning through her mind like blind lab rats in an endless maze. She closed the refrigerator. Still, it was unsettling to find Joe Mitchum occupying her thoughts so fully. What had changed?

Nothing. He was gifted at getting in trouble, and this time his foolish behavior had nearly gotten him killed. She'd performed her job by resuscitating him. That was it. Her noisome neighbor was intriguing only from a medical standpoint. That's why she'd spent hours on the computer last night searching medical databases for information on lightning strike survivors.

The facts had amazed her. In the United States alone, twelve hundred people a year were hit by lightning. Less than ten percent of the victims died, so from a statistical standpoint, it wasn't miraculous that Joe had survived. That a trained doctor happened to be near enough to begin CPR immediately? Probably a coincidence. Or Joe's dumb luck.

He would have suffered respiratory failure, followed quickly by cardiac arrest if the chain of events had been different. She couldn't shake the idea that she'd been thrust on the scene for a reason.

With nothing to occupy her time once the housework was done, Mallory gave in to a strange compulsion to drive to the hospital and check on Joe's progress. When she arrived, she discovered he'd been moved from ICU into a regular bed on third floor medical. She stopped by the nurses' station to skim his chart and read the latest lab reports. Everything was normal. As were his vital signs. No indication of infection in the burns on his feet.

Modern medicine, one. Mother Nature, zero.

She was about to close the chart when one of Mac's nota-
tions caught her eye: Mental status exams inconclusive for
residual cognitive impairment. However, nursing staff reports
episodes of confusion and disorientation. Consider neurological referral if condition persists.

Before she could ask the nurse on duty about those episodes, the doctor stepped into the cubicle on his evening
rounds. He'd been kind enough to drive her home after she'd
ridden to the hospital in the ambulance with Joe.

"Hey, Mallory, what are you doing here?" He pulled a
patient's chart from the rack and flipped it open to jot a quick
note. "I thought one of the perks of being a clinic doc was
no weekend duty."

"Just checking on Mitchum." She closed the chart and patted it. "Sounds like he's doing all right."

"Physically. He appears to have suffered some memory
loss, but considering what he's been through, his recovery has
been amazing. In fact, I'm ready to discharge him."

She shot him a questioning glance, and he shrugged. "No
insurance. I'm catching flak from the business office to cut
him loose."

Mallory groaned. Mac knew her opinion of the early release
policy for indigent patients. She turned to the nurse seated
nearby. "Good news for the staff, huh? I don't imagine
Mitchum is a very pleasant patient."

When Nurse Evelyn Dodd looked up, her apple dumpling
face was etched with surprise. "Are you kidding? Joe's a
sweetheart. A real pleasure to have on the floor. Such a gentleman." The middle-aged nurse pulled homemade treats
wrapped in cellophane from the stash in her bottom drawer
and offered them to the docs. "Here, you two look hungry.
Actually, I'll be sorry to see him go."

Now it was Mallory's turn to act surprised. Sweetheart and
gentleman were not words she would have chosen to describe
Joe Mitchum. "Really? That's interesting."

"He hasn't had a single visitor," Evelyn went on. "I asked
if he wanted me to contact anyone, and he said there was no

one to call. That just breaks my heart. A nice boy like that ought to have lots of folks worried about him.''

Nice boy? ''We *are* talking about Joe Mitchum, right?'' Mallory could believe the loner had no friends or relatives concerned about his well-being. He'd managed to alienate just about everyone who'd ever tried to have a relationship with him. The thing she found hard to accept was the nurse's generous assessment of his personality. And the fact that he hadn't summoned any of his bottom-feeder female companions to his bedside.

''Yeah, he's not as bad as you made him out to be, Mal.'' Mac finished charting and returned the file to the rack. ''You had me expecting a dumb oaf with the IQ of a keg of lug nuts. Instead, he's soft-spoken and polite. Pretty sharp, too, considering how close his brain came to frying like a funnel cake.''

''What gets me is he's so grateful for every little thing we do for him.'' Evelyn wiped a tear from her eye. ''It's embarrassing. I keep telling him I'm just doing my job. Speaking of which…'' she slipped her stethoscope around her neck. ''I've got vitals to check. You docs be good now.''

Mac bit into Evelyn's brownie and rolled his eyes in bliss. ''Mmm, delicious.'' He noticed her watching him and sighed. ''What?''

Mallory shook her head. ''That just doesn't make sense. I did some research on lightning strike survivors and didn't find a single case where being charged with 100 million volts of electricity actually improved the victim's personality.''

Mac laughed. ''You never know. Maybe rubbing elbows with the Grim Reaper made the guy turn over a new leaf.''

''Hmph! Joe Mitchum would have to turn over a whole forest to achieve sweetheart status.''

Mac poked the last of the brownie in his mouth and held out his hand for Joe's chart. ''I'm writing the discharge order. I don't have any medical reason to keep him, and I've already told him he could go home.''

''What about the 'episodes of confusion and disorientation' I read about?'' Mallory fidgeted in the swivel chair. Sitting still was difficult. New nervous energy made her want to keep moving. Moving toward Joe. Disgusted by the thought, she forced herself back to reason.

Mac looked up from his note-writing. "Taking a jolt like that would give anyone a memory lapse. Didn't your research turn that up?"

"Well, yeah." Her reading had revealed a broad range of lightning effects. Victims often sustained skull fractures, ruptured eardrums, bruises on the heart, brain contusions and paralyzed lungs, among other things.

"He does fine on cognitive tests, but seems to have a few word finding problems and trouble recalling past events."

"What about the neurological referral?"

"I told him if he's still having problems in a week or two to let me know. I'd appreciate it if you'd keep an eye on him for me."

"Me?"

"Isn't that what neighbors are for?"

"Please."

"Are you going to eat that?" Mac eyed the brownie she'd forgotten.

Mallory handed it over. "If you're planning to remain a confirmed bachelor forever, you really should learn to cook."

"No time."

"I think I'll look in on Joe before I leave." Mallory made the decision sound professional. In truth, she'd had a weird urge to see him all weekend. What was the matter with her?

Walking down the hall, she gently pushed open the door to his room and watched his clumsy efforts to make the bed for a moment before speaking. "You don't have to do that, you know."

At the sound of her voice, he stopped trying to smooth the blanket and turned, leaning on a pair of aluminum crutches. When he saw her, his face creased in a wide, happy grin. "Mol-Mallory! I mean, ma'am. Dr. Peterson. Lordy, I don't know what to call you." He grasped the crutches and turned, leaning awkwardly against the bed.

It took Mallory a moment to respond. The lightning bolt

had left quite a transformation in its wake. He was clean-shaven for the first time in as long as she could remember. His shaggy hair had been clipped short. A do-it-yourself job, judging from the uneven results. She noticed tiny flecks of gray gleaming among the dark strands. Were those new?

"You can call me Mallory. We go back far enough for that."

"Yes." He nodded and gave her a small, enigmatic smile. "We do." He must have noticed her staring at his clothes. "Nurse Evelyn showed me the outfit I was wearing when I got here. Everything was so tattered, it looked like I was the loser in a bear fight."

"Yes, that happens sometimes with lightning. Clothing is shredded, metal zippers and fasteners fuse. People have been knocked right out of their shoes."

"She said the owners wouldn't be needing these now." He was dressed in a pair of freshly laundered jeans and a wrinkled white shirt that had been washed but not ironed. "I don't know about wearing a dead man's clothes, but since I was pretty near dead myself, maybe they won't bring me bad luck."

"I don't think you have to worry about that."

"I reckon not. I've been plenty lucky lately."

Reckon? Hardly a Joe word. Now that she thought about it, he sounded different too. The timbre of his voice had changed. It was deeper, more confident. Temporary inflammation of the trachea maybe.

That wouldn't account for the change in his eyes. Where before they had been mud-dark and flat, the luminous brown depths now possessed an indefinable mystery. As if that weren't unsettling enough, there was also a new stillness in his features. Surely, such composure hadn't been there before. Just looking at him was like glimpsing the familiar for the first time. Like what Brindon's wife Dorian had said about the Eiffel Tower. The image had been imprinted on her consciousness for so long that when she finally saw it, she had felt an eerie sense of recognition.

Joe's straight nose, firm lips and dimpled chin were the same. Yet, they were different, too. Finer. Like a stone tumbled by a river, until all its rough edges had been worn smooth. Why had she never noticed how good-looking he was? A twist of shame tightened her belly. Maybe she'd never really looked at him before. Never truly listened. Never given him a chance.

Her character flaws didn't explain how he had morphed from a greasy, ill-mannered slacker into a clean soft-spoken man who said "reckon" and "ma'am" and endeared himself to career nurses. Now *there* was a mystery.

"Seriously. You don't have to make the bed. They have people to do that."

"Seems the least I can do, considering everything folks have done for me. They bring me tasty grub three times a day and juice and cookies whether I want 'em or not. Some lady's always coming in to check my temperature and make sure I'm comfortable. It sure is a hospitable place. Hmm...guess that's why they call it a hospital, huh?"

"Maybe so." Mallory smiled, but his comments confused her. He was sincere, not flippant or sarcastic. Sincerity was not an attitude she expected from a man who had been born obnoxious and then suffered numerous relapses. "Dr. McKinley tells me you're ready to go home."

"Yep. As nice as it is here, I can't afford to run up a bill for room and board." He gestured to the bedside chair. "Would you care to have a seat?"

Mallory sat, marveling at his courtesy. The last time she'd seen him, he had suggested she buy a six-pack and watch a wrestling match. "Has anyone talked to you about your bill?"

"Yes, ma'am. A nice lady came in. Called herself a social worker. How can she be social and work at the same time?" He shrugged. "Said they'd fix me up with a payment plan so I can settle my debt when I get back on my feet."

"Good. How are you planning to get home? Have you called someone to come for you?" Mallory tried not to stare, but was intrigued by the way the setting sun shone through the window and backlit his head with a golden corona.

"No. There's no one I care to call. Since I'm afoot, I guess I'll walk it."

"On those?" She eyed the crutches propped against the

bed. "Excuse me for saying so, but you haven't exactly mastered their use."

He grimaced apologetically. "I'm about as gimpy as a one-legged chicken. Dr. Mac said I should keep off my feet for a few days, but I figure I can make it home."

"Slapdown's twenty miles from here," she reminded him.

"It is? Well, of course it is. Maybe hoofing isn't the way to go."

"I can give you a ride home."

His face brightened, his warm brown eyes glowing with appreciation. "I'd be much obliged."

She echoed Mac's words. "What are neighbors for?"

"We're neighbors?"

Was this an example of the confusion the nurses had noted? "You live next door to the clinic where I work and close to where I live."

He beamed. "Well, good. That's about the best news I've heard all day."

News? Had he forgotten where he lived? "Really, Joe, how are you feeling?"

"Right as rain and happy as a pup with two tails."

Brain damage was definitely a possibility. Simply being charged with negative electrons wouldn't cause him to suddenly start talking like a character from Mayberry. "Are you sure?"

"Matter of fact, I haven't felt this alive in…well, let's just say in a long, long time."

A couple of hours later Joe checked himself out of the hospital, and they drove home. Dodging Mallory's questions was like walking through a cow pasture: you had to watch where you stepped. He couldn't tell if she was suspicious about him or just abnormally curious. The only good thing about living through lightning was having an excuse to act as worn-out as a fat uncle's welcome.

He pretended to wake up when Mallory parked her little truck in front of a rickety metal house on wheels. From the beat-up look of it, the trailer as Mallory called it, had been plunked down in the middle of the junk-strewn lot by a cy-clone. Several skinny dogs crawled out of the shade to bark a yapping welcome. Joe's heart sank deeper as he looked around. "I live here?"

Mallory grimaced. "Home sweet home. I fed the demon horde while you were in the hospital."

"The what?"

"The dogs."

"Oh. Thank you." He looked around in disgust. What kind of self-respecting man lived in a rat-hole like this? The place would embarrass a blind fur trapper. "Are all these dogs mine?"

"Apparently so. Five at last count."

"That's a heap of dog."

"And not a keeper in the bunch."

Joe reached for the door handle, and grinned when he knew exactly how the contraption worked. That happened more often than not. As Celestian had predicted, his new body carried the old Joe's physical memories. Deeply ingrained in his sinews, they enabled him to adapt to his new life without going walleyed over twenty-first century advancements. That's why watching television and walking through automatic doors and racing along the road at more than fifty miles per hour didn't feel nearly as strange as it should have.

"Thanks for the ride," he told Mallory. "If you'll fetch my crutches from the back, I'll get on in the...house."

"Shall I help you out of the truck?"

"I can manage." She handed him the crutches, and he hopped onto the uneven ground. Pain zinged up his legs from the burns on the soles of his bandaged feet. He hoped the inside of his new home wasn't as junked up as the outside. If it were, he'd have a heck of a time getting around.

Mallory walked ahead and opened the door. He limped across the yard, and the hounds slunk up to sniff him. A couple growled and backed off, while the rest tucked their tails and whimpered back into their hiding places. None of them seemed exactly enraptured to see him.

"So much for man's best friends, huh?" Mallory held the

door open. "Leave for a couple of days, and they forget who you are."

Joe struggled onto the cinder block that served as a step, and Mallory took his arm to help him inside. He ducked under the low threshold, and a powerful stink slapped him in the face. "Whoa! It smells worse in here than hell on house-cleaning day."

Mallory stepped inside and poked around the tiny kitchen until she discovered the source of the stench. "Sheesh, Mitchum! You left a pound of hamburger in the fridge, and the electricity's been off all weekend."

With her hand clamped over her nose, she couldn't have looked more disgusted if she'd uncovered a decaying corpse. "You can't stay. The place is filthy. There's no telling what kind of infection you'd contract just walking around in here."

"I reckon I can clean things up."

"You and what hazmat team? There's no power, no running water and it's hotter than a brick oven. No one should live like this."

Being from west Texas, he didn't mind the heat, though a smart man could learn to like the cool air they had at the hospital. He wouldn't miss electricity and running water. Such luxuries had been beyond his ranger's salary. That toe-curling smell, though, would take some getting used to.

"C'mon, let's get out of here." Mallory found a couple of brown paper bags. Into one, she stuffed clothes from the tiny wardrobe and built-in drawers. She dropped the rotting pack-age of meat into the other and carried it outside, flinging it into a charred metal barrel. "I hope those mutts don't turn over the trash can."

"Might improve the looks of the place." Joe leaned on the crutches and limped down the step. "Where are we going?"

Mallory tossed his makeshift suitcase in the back of the truck and helped him into the passenger seat. "I have an extra room. You can stay with me until the bandages come off, and you can walk without crutches."

Her offer confused him. "I don't know about that. How

will it look for a young maiden lady to take a man into her home?''

She laughed. "A young what?"

"I couldn't forgive myself if I besmirched your reputation in any way."

She glanced sideways at him as she started the engine and shifted gears. "You're kidding, right?"

The blast of cool air from the dashboard was a modern convenience he would hate to give up. "I know how people talk."

"Don't worry about my reputation, Mitchum, I can take care of myself. And don't get any smart ideas. I'm offering you a place to stay. Nothing else."

"Well, if you're sure it won't get you into hot water."

"Let me ask you something." She threw the gearshift back into Park and turned to face him. "Since when have you been so concerned about what people think?" Her golden eyes flashed, and her full lips clamped together in a don't-lie-to-me line.

"A good reputation is the most valuable thing a person can own," he replied.

"Is that a fact?"

"Yes, ma'am. I'd rather lose my right arm than my honor."

Her sudden hoot of laughter wounded him in a way he hadn't known possible. He fell silent in the face of her ridicule. The old Joe must have lived by a different code. That's why Mallory held him in such low esteem. An obstacle like that would complicate his mission, but sharing living quarters with her would provide him with plenty of opportunities to win her over.

He watched Mallory angle the gearshift into Reverse and back out of the rutted drive. He couldn't see Molly in her face, but at times, he could hear his old love in her words, sense her in Mallory's efficient movements. Not now of course. At the moment, she was all Mallory. A smart woman who wouldn't admit there were things she couldn't understand. A familiar stranger who would never know how important she was to him unless he opened her eyes.

He wouldn't lose this chance. He was meant to be here and felt at peace in Mallory's company. He felt like a man who'd finally made it home after a long, heart-sore journey.

When he and Celestian hadn't been biting each other's heads off, they'd had deep discussions. A hundred years added up to a lot of gab. One topic they'd thrashed out was the purpose of corporeal life.

The Spirit-Maker divided every created spirit and sent it on an earthly mission to find its other half. The Plan provided each questing spirit with the knowledge needed to complete its search. However, due to a snag in the system, once a spirit assumed human form, it seemed to forget its mission. Human beings expended enormous time and energy creating philosophies and religions to explain their existence. But what they didn't know—couldn't know—was that when they made the right connection, everything else fell into place.

A whole spirit could change the world, do unlimited good, serve the Spirit-Maker and mankind. A half spirit could only quest. And while that spirit might accomplish worthwhile objectives on earth, it would never feel complete as it yearned forever for its missing half.

Without even knowing what it hungered for.

Hope was eternal, and if a half-life spirit alighted in Reception, it was carefully rerouted to begin the cycle again. Considering how important the quest was in the scheme of things, it was an ironically sad fact of cosmic life that only a few managed to find the spirit that would make them whole. All were given the opportunity, but most were too blind to use it.

The Ranger considered himself lucky. He'd spent several lifetimes with his healer half and then a century in time-out, learning the way. Fate had handed him an undeserved gift when it allowed him to return as Mallory's neighbor. He was not going to make the most human of all mistakes and forfeit his last chance.

Because of the old Joe's poor housekeeping habits, he could spend the next few days under the same roof as his destiny. Things were looking up. Coincidences that weren't coincidences had come to his aid.

Mallory steered the truck into the paved parking lot, drove past the clinic, and up a little hill. She parked in front of a white house with green shutters, surrounded with neat flowerbeds and trimmed grass. Potted plants swung from the porch posts. This was more like it. This was a home, not a hovel. Good things could happen here.

He sighed gratefully.

Thank you, Joe Mitchum, wherever you are, for being such a lazy ne'er-do-well.

Chapter Three

Mallory settled Joe in an extra bedroom at the opposite end of the house. He would have his own bathroom, so their paths would not have to cross any more than necessary. So far, he hadn't been nearly as annoying as she knew he could be, but once the shock wore off, he might revert to old habits.

Openly admiring the accommodations, he limped around the blue-and-white bedroom on his crutches, pulling out drawers and inspecting the closet. He bounced the mattress experimentally with one hand and grinned like he'd never seen a pillow-top queen before. Some people were easily impressed.

She left him to put away the things she'd grabbed at the trailer while she started dinner. She hadn't been her practical, logical self since that errant bolt of lightning had thrust Joe Mitchum into her life. Doing something mundane would restore her sense of normalcy. Making nice with a guy whom she'd always considered an odious nuisance was unnerving. Factor in the twitchiness that overcame her when he was near, and it was no wonder she was feeling weird.

Helping Joe was a way of paying back some of the generosity she'd received over the years. A distressing mission of mercy, but somebody had to do it. Hoping he wouldn't give her a reason to regret opening her home to him, she heated water for spaghetti and dumped a bag of prepackaged salad into a bowl. Turning to the stove with pasta for the boiling pot, she jumped and nearly dropped it. Joe was watching her intently from the doorway.

"Jeepers! Don't sneak up on me like that! Do you want to give *me* cardiac arrest?" After years of living alone, having another person around would take some getting used to. Having Joe Mitchum around…well, there were some things she would never get used to.

"I didn't mean to startle you." He leaned on his crutches and took in the gleaming appliances, glass-fronted cupboards and cheerful sunflower wallpaper. "Nice place."

"Thanks, but it's not mine." She melted butter for garlic bread. "Remember? Housing is a perk I get for working at the clinic."

"Oh, right. I forgot."

He'd forgotten a lot of things. He hadn't seemed to recognize much when they'd driven through town. She'd left him in the truck while she ran into the grocery store to pick up a few things. When she came out, Glorieta Tadlock was leaning in the passenger window attempting to engage him in conversation. In the loosest sense of the word. Dressed in a sequined halter-top that showed off the butterfly tattoo on her shoulder and short shorts that showed off everything else, the blowzy blonde treated him like a baby bird that had fallen out of its nest. To Joe's credit, he'd seemed perplexed and embarrassed by the attention.

If she hadn't known better, Mallory would have sworn he'd never laid eyes on the belly-ringed nail technician in his life. Which was pretty strange considering the two had once been an item. Since neither knew what the word platonic meant, he'd probably laid a lot more than his eyes on her.

"So you can live here as long as you're the doc?" he asked.

"Or until I get a place of my own." Before she did that, she planned to save enough to put a down payment on a house for her parents. Seeing their only child through medical school had cracked their working-class nest egg. Buying them a home

wouldn't come close to repaying all the sacrifices they'd made
for her, but at least they wouldn't have to worry about the
future.

Happily married for nearly forty years, Al and Lois Peterson
had set a good example of wedded bliss for their daughter.
Unfortunately, Mallory had never had time to be much of a
romantic and didn't believe she would ever find the kind of
love her parents shared. Her doubts weren't based on logic,
they just *were*. She'd never suffered a betrayal. No faithless
lover had broken her heart. She simply didn't think of herself
and true love in the same context.

She assumed it was because she'd always been too focused
on her goals to fall in love. College and medical school and
interning had made it impossible to fit a personal life into her
schedule. She had more time now, but neither the inclination
nor opportunity. A drought of available men had just about
dried up the gene pool in Slapdown.

At the age of twenty-nine, solitude had become a habit.

"I hope your room is all right." She set the salad bowl on
the table. The careful way he watched her increased her jitters.
It was one thing not to find him totally repugnant, but finding
him intriguing and attractive was like slipping into an alternate
universe.

"It's more than all right. This is just about the swankiest
place I've ever stayed."

Mallory smiled. He thought a doublewide on a wind-swept
west Texas hill was swanky? Poor man didn't get out much.
"Why don't you have a seat? Dinner's almost ready."

He stood in the doorway, looking uneasy. "I wouldn't feel
right sitting down before you."

"Don't be silly, get off those feet. Doctor's orders."

Reluctantly, he pulled out a chair and levered himself into
it. He bumped his left foot against the table leg and winced.

"If you're hurting, I've got pain reliever."

"I've known worse."

Odd. Stoicism was another quality she'd never associated
with Joe. He'd probably caused more pain than he'd ever experienced. She thought of the people he'd hurt most of all.

"You can use the phone to call Brandy if you want. Maybe you should let your family know where you are?"

A look of panic flashed in his eyes before he shuttered them from her scrutiny. "No. I don't think so."

Oh. Sore spot. Mentioning the ex-wife wasn't the way to go. "Whatever you think is best." The couple had been divorced over a year, but Mallory's mother stayed current on town gossip despite her recent retirement from the diner, and said the marriage had ended long before that. Brandy had told Mallory at Chloe's last clinic appointment that she was trying to make a new start by getting into paralegal school.

Mallory drained the pasta and poured a jar of sauce over it. After placing it on a slow burner to warm, she removed the Italian bread from the oven. Joe followed her movements as though trying to memorize them. Why? Unless his memory loss was more serious than Mac suspected, he surely knew how to make spaghetti the easy way. Long a master of deception, Joe might have faked his way through the tests, fooling the doctor into thinking he was doing better than he was.

Conducting a little covert evaluation of her own shouldn't be too difficult. After all, he wasn't going anywhere for the next few days.

She served the food and was flabbergasted when Joe bowed his head over his plate. Manners *and* religion? No way. Things were getting downright spooky around here. First thing tomorrow morning she was checking Dink Potter's alfalfa field for crop circles. She followed his example, echoing his heartfelt "amen" at the end of the silent thanksgiving.

"Looks good," he said enthusiastically as he picked up his fork. "What's it called?"

"Spaghetti." Another word-finding lapse. Maybe the nurses were right to be concerned. They spent more time with patients than doctors, and their astute observations were usually dead-on. "You seem different to me, Joe." She took a sip of ice tea.

"Do I?" He kept his eyes on his food. Good thing. Their new harrowing, hypnotic quality gave her the shivers.

"Just a little." Like maybe scouts from an alien mothership

had sucked out the old Joe and replaced him with a too-perfect pod person.

"I reckon I'm still a little befuddled."

Befuddled? There was another term you didn't hear every day. His expressive language problems hadn't affected his newly acquired vocabulary of Mayberryisms. "I've noticed you have some trouble remembering things."

"I suppose. They tell me I had quite a jolt."

"To put it mildly." Shock. Temporary cardiopulmonary failure. Oxygen deprivation. A fluid-filled body was an excellent conductor of electricity. Lightning entered through holes in the head, eyes, nose, ears and mouth. The brain, bathed in salt water, was particularly vulnerable to electrical effects. The fact that he was sitting here talking at all was amazing.

She poured bottled dressing on her salad. "Ranch or French?"

He looked up, clearly confused by the question. She raised one brow, waiting for his answer.

"Neither." Joe continued wrangling the slippery spaghetti onto his fork.

Fast thinking. She'd seen stroke patients become quite proficient at compensating for cognitive deficits. The smart ones learned quickly how to talk around the odd little holes in their memory. Like calling a hammer a hitter and using verbal confabulation to avoid answering direct questions. She'd try another tack. "Would you like dressing on your salad?"

He looked up, and a large blob of sauce-soaked pasta slid off his fork into his lap. "Tarnation!" He grabbed for his napkin, upsetting his glass in the process. Tea and ice cubes joined the spaghetti. "Well, now I've done it!"

Mallory stepped over to the rack near the sink and tore off a wad of paper towels, which she handed to him. He scooped up the spaghetti, and then scrubbed at the wet tomato stain on the front of his jeans.

"I'm as clumsy as a booze-blind cowboy." Flushing, he dabbed at the puddle of tea darkening the green placemat. "I hope I didn't ruin anything."

She stood beside him, trying not to let her gaze linger too long on the disaster area. "You need to get those pants off."

"I *beg* your pardon?" He looked genuinely shocked.

Since "inappropriate" best described his former communication style, she hadn't realized he possessed a moral sensibility, or that it could be easily offended. "Your jeans? You need to take them off so I can work on the stain. Otherwise it'll set and never come out."

"Oh." He seemed relieved by her lack of ulterior motives. "I'll go change. You can't wash them tonight."

"Why not?"

"I want you to finish your supper first."

"They can wash while we eat."

He left the room shaking his head. When he returned, he was wearing a pair of dark blue work pants. Why he owned such a garment when work wasn't something he did on a regular basis was beyond her. She carried the stained jeans to the laundry closet off the kitchen, sprayed them with prewash and dropped them into the churning machine.

Again, Joe seemed a little too impressed by an everyday process. "So that's all there is to it?"

"To stain removal, you mean?"

"To laundry." He seemed so amazed.

"Yeah, I haven't had to pound clothes on a flat rock down at the stream for quite a while now." She laughed at her joke, but he didn't seem to get it. He stood until she sat down. "Let's try this again. Do you want salad dressing?"

"Thank you, I would."

"Ranch or French?"

He paused as if needing another hint. She picked up the two bottles and waggled them. Understanding finally dawned. "The red one."

"Okay. Now we're getting somewhere."

Joe had never felt so incompetent in his life. Celestian had spent too much time telling him what *not* to do, and not nearly enough explaining what he *should* do. He was expected to know people he'd never heard of, like the half-dressed floozy at the market. Was she one of Joe's friends? Or worse yet, was she *more* than a friend? If it was true that you could judge a man by the company he kept, he was in deep trouble.

Then there was Brandy. Mallory said she was family. What if Joe had relatives around? A mother would surely recognize her own son. At the very least, she'd realize a stranger had stowed away in his body. Why hadn't he considered the past associations angle? Why hadn't Celestian?

People were not the worst of his problems. Everything had changed during the hundred years he'd spent cooling his heels in the time-out room. He was flopping around like a trout out of water. Even though he'd observed the passage of time on the spirit monitor and had tried to catch up by watching television in the hospital, seeing and doing were two different things.

Oh, there had been telephones and automobiles and moving pictures in his day. But now people carried phones in their pockets, drove cars that could go over 100 miles an hour and instead of buying a ticket to watch a show, they bought the whole danged thing and took it home. Traveling by air had still been a dream when he'd last left earth. Hard as it was to believe, common folks now flew all the time, and men had walked on the moon.

He hadn't believed anything as basic as food could change, but it had. Not only was it different, it was better and more abundant. You could enjoy an orange year around, not just at Christmas. Driving home today, Mallory had stopped at a mercantile called a supermarket. It was full of all kinds of food, and people could walk in and buy whatever they wanted if they had the money. No planting seeds, no hoeing weeds. No backbreaking harvest when crops were good, no starving when they didn't thrive. Families no longer had to grow their own foodstuff because the agricultural industry did it for them.

Realizing how much the world had changed only reminded him of the gap between Mallory and himself. He had so much to learn, so many obstacles to overcome. Hoping he was up to the task, he returned his attention to his plate. Spaghetti was tasty enough, but it was tricky, and a man had to work too hard for it. He tried following Mallory's lead by twirling the strands around his fork but ended up dropping more than he ate. After battling the perfidious noodles for several more minutes, he gave up and went to work on the French-dressed salad. He'd never been much on eating raw greens, but at least they didn't put up much of a fight.

His ineptness had aroused Mallory's suspicions. Maybe it wasn't a good idea to stay with her after all. She was bound to figure out something was wrong, and when she did, there would be hell to pave and no hot pitch. His main chance was convincing her the lightning had scrambled his thoughts. As a doctor, she was apt to believe that before she would the truth.

A truth he wasn't allowed to tell.

He helped himself to another piece of buttery bread, hoping to sop up some of his hunger. He'd just about danced his last step with spaghetti.

When he finished, Mallory collected his plate. "Would you like some pudding for dessert?"

"Too much trouble. I wouldn't want to put you out."

She smiled. "Hmm. Could mean yes. Could mean no. Why don't you simplify things and pick one for me?"

"Yes, I'd like pudding. Please." He'd always loved sweets. Molly had chided him about sucking on hard candies and dumping two spoons of sugar in his coffee.

Mallory opened the icebox and removed three little cups, all attached to each other. With the flick of a wrist, she snapped one off and handed it to him. "Hope you like chocolate."

"My favorite." Unsure how to open the cup, he waited until she revealed the trick, then peeled back the foil top and spooned up the creamy contents.

His mother had made chocolate pudding for him when he was a kid back on the farm, but the process had been more complicated. His father had grown the hay to feed the cow his mother milked. After straining the squeezings, she'd mixed in sugar and cocoa powder and cornstarch. After chopping wood for the fire, she'd stood over the hot stove for twenty minutes, stirring until her arm ached so the contents wouldn't scorch. He'd had to wait for the bowl to cool in the window before he could eat his treat, still warm and rich and sweet.

He clung to the memory. Celestian might have been vague about the details of walking-in, but he'd warned that the more time he spent as Joe, the less he would remember of his last life. Details would become misty and eventually dry up like dew in the morning sun. After a while, he would have no more recollection of his life as Will Pendleton than he had of the many others he'd lived. Memories were normally deleted in the rebirth cycle, but walking-in bypassed the process. As a result, recollections of his former life would slowly fade away, forcing him to experience all the pain of their loss.

He finished his dessert and watched as Mallory tossed the empty containers in the trash. Amazing how technology had eliminated so many steps in something as simple as a bowl of pudding. A person didn't even have to touch a cow nowadays. It was just snap-peel-eat and don't save the dish!

"It's still early," Mallory said as she stacked their dirty plates in a machine under the counter. "What would you like to do? I can show you some of the information dealing with lightning strike research on the computer."

Sensing she planned to do more than share information, he begged off. He wasn't up to taking a test tonight. "I'm running down faster than a two dollar watch. If you don't mind, I'd like to turn in." As much as he wanted to spend time with her, he feared fatigue would trip him up. He might say the wrong thing and make her even more suspicious. She already thought Joe was different. He couldn't let her know how much.

"I understand. If you need anything, let me know." She pushed a button on the dishwashing machine, and it whirred to life, cleaning behind a closed door. Modern folks had come up with all kinds of marvelous contraptions to make their lives easy. But in doing so they had distanced themselves from the very life they were trying to improve. Toilets flushed, washers removed stains and unseen hands picked vegetables and killed meat. What did people do with all the time their wondrous inventions saved?

Tired as he was, Joe couldn't sleep. He lay in the wide bed in the dark, his head filled with disturbing images. There was a good reason prior life memories were wiped clean. Some things weren't meant to be recalled.

Like dying three days before your wedding and being stuck in the time-out room to watch your beloved grieve. The only thing worse was failing to leap the breach at all and spending eternity as a bereft, earthbound spirit. An uncommon occurrence, but it happened.

He tried to concentrate on Mallory and formulate a plan to keep himself out of trouble. When he couldn't think of one, he decided to tell her tomorrow he was returning to the rattletrap trailer. Living in his own place was safer, even if it smelled worse than a sheepherder's socks.

He hated to leave Mallory. Just being in the same room with her was a joy. How he'd ached to touch her tonight. To push that stubborn curl out of her eyes. It had taken considerable willpower to head for his room when all he wanted was to be near her.

She filled his senses and his thoughts, but that didn't stop him from thinking about the woman she'd once been. The two were tied together in his heart. If Celestian was right about his past life fading, he had to sort out his thoughts before he lost his Molly memories.

Molly Earnshaw had been a corker. Strong and independent, she'd taken the news of his untimely passing hard. Donning a black dress, she arranged a nice funeral for him. Lots of people showed up, telling her how sorry they were and how it was a crying shame when the good died young. He didn't have a lot of friends in his old life; warrior spirits maintained few ties. But he'd earned the respect of everyone he knew, and they all turned out to see him off.

Through it all, Molly stood straight, her pretty-plain face composed and solemn. However, at night when she was alone, she wept hard into her pillow. She sent up prayer after prayer, seeking understanding or at the very least, acceptance. She had lost some of her faith when those prayers had not been answered to her satisfaction. Feeling responsible for her anguish, he had closed his eyes against the scene on the spirit monitor.

Molly never married. How could she when she'd lost the love of her life too soon? After a long mourning year, folks had tried to convince her to give love another chance. She'd turned away from their well-meaning interference and from men who hoped to court her. She'd wrapped herself in the spinster life, wearing it like a woolen shawl that insulated her feelings. She had never taken off the engagement ring Will Pendleton had slipped on her finger. She'd dressed in black for the rest of her lonely life, grieving for her other half until she'd departed her worn-out mortal coil.

That was why he'd jumped at the chance to return to earth, even if he had to do so by unconventional means. Warriors were driven to make things right. In every life, he'd battled injustice in its many forms. Dying before his time had been his fate, but eternal loneliness shouldn't have been Molly's.

She was gone now, beyond his help. But he had to try and relieve the burden her healer spirit had carried into her present life. Giving and caring toward others, Mallory didn't believe in true love. The loss she'd suffered in Molly's lifetime wouldn't let her. She didn't understand why she was still blocking the pain, but he did.

Her human heart had stopped seeking before it had even begun.

Residual Effect was what happened when events in one existence influenced behavior in the next. He'd felt its effects often enough. Though he couldn't know for sure, he suspected many lives ago, he had lost his honor and suffered greatly for it. Residual Effect explained why he was compelled to preserve honor at all costs.

From what he'd seen so far, ideals like honor and responsibility hadn't been very important to Joe Mitchum. He would have a long row to hoe to redeem himself in Mallory's eyes. A daunting task, but he was up to it. Because until he earned her respect, he could never hope to win her love.

Chapter Four

Mallory was charting in her office the next day when she heard Joe's dog pack barking across the fence. Barking? Try raising an unholy racket. Barking was normal. A canine response to perceived danger. The uproar next door was anything but. Unless the mangy mutts were trying to alert the county to an imminent alien invasion.

Unable to see the cause of the commotion from her window, she hurried out to reception and found the waiting room deserted. Muzak played to an empty house. No patients at 4:45 on a Monday afternoon? Okay. Now she knew something strange was going on.

"Jeannie? Did we not get the memo about the world coming to an end?"

The forty-something office manager looked up from her computer. "We've covered all the appointments for the day. Weird, huh?"

"Very." Crop circle weird. Call the record book people weird. Gentleman Joe weird. Mondays were always the busiest days at the clinic because people who got sick over the weekend wanted to see the doctor. She usually worked until 7:00 p.m., but on Mondays, it could be much later. "Have you noticed any Sasquatch tracks on the lawn? Any low-flying objects you couldn't readily identify?''

"Don't look a gift unicorn in the mouth, boss," Jeannie admonished. "Can I leave when I get this paperwork done?''

"Sure. Go home. Early Mondays come along about as often as comets and eclipses.'' The dogs' persistent yapping reminded her why she'd left her office in the first place. "What's up next door?''

"I dunno.'' Jeannie stepped from behind the counter and the two women walked outside.

"What the heck?'' Shading her eyes against the bright afternoon sun, Mallory quickly spotted the source of the dogs' alarm. A big red tow truck was backed up to Joe's trailer. The driver appeared to be readying it for transport. The demon horde, willing to yap and growl as long as they didn't actually have to defend the place, made half-hearted forays around the truck, nipping at the tires and putting on a grand show.

"Looks like it's *sayonara* for the trash can on wheels.'' Jeannie did an NFL victory dance. "This really is our lucky day.''

"Who would do such a thing?'' Dread clunked to the pit of Mallory's stomach. They couldn't haul away Joe's home. Where would he live when his burns healed? Certainly not with her. Their arrangement was temporary. A couple of days. No more.

Jeannie grinned. "I believe you were the one who complained to the town council about Joe's place, Doc. Nice to know citizens still have a voice in municipal government, huh?''

"I gotta find out what's going on.'' She slipped off her lab coat and hung it inside on a hook by the door before taking off at a lope.

Jeannie's laughter followed her out to the parking lot. "Hey, Doc, since you seem to have so much influence, why don't you put a bug in the animal control guy's ear, too?''

Mallory sprinted across the field separating Joe's trailer from the clinic. Tall grass embedded tiny, sticky seed heads in her white cotton socks. She should have used the driveway, but this was a code blue situation. The grimly efficient tow-truck driver looked like a man on a mission.

"Hey! Mister!" She ran the last few yards clutching her side. "What do you think you're doing?"

The lanky driver, past fifty and with a thin face to match the rest of his body, consulted a greasy impound order. "Says here I'm supposed to remove a code-deficient recreational vehicle, which would be that." Without looking up, he pointed to the trailer. "From property on the west side of Wooster Road near Western Plains Clinic, which would be there." He pointed to her building. "And transport it to the R & W Salvage Yard, which would be thataway." He jabbed a finger in the appropriate direction. He looked up from his reading. "That's what I'm doing."

"By whose order?" she panted.

Early, according to the name tape sewn above his pocket, consulted his paperwork again. "That would be the mayor."

"But why?"

"From the looks of the place, I reckon somebody complained."

"That would be me." She echoed his deadpan delivery. "But I just wanted the council to make him clean up and get rid of some of the junk."

Early took a slow, assessing look around, then spit a stream of brown tobacco juice on the ground. "So what's the problem? I'm taking the biggest piece of junk with me when I leave."

"But where will he live?"

Early shrugged. "Don't know." And judging by the heartless disregard with which he hitched Joe's trailer to his truck, he didn't much care.

Careful to stay out of kicking range, the dogs' annoying yipping reached fever pitch. Mallory stamped her foot. "Oh, for Pete's sake. Shut up!"

And they did. Five pairs of idiot eyes looked at her as if to say, "Gee, lady, all you had to do was ask." Her ears were still ringing as she appealed to Early's humanitarianism. "Look. I'm the doctor at the clinic. The owner of this trailer just survived being struck by lightning. He nearly died. He's recovering from second-degree burns and…probable brain damage. If you impound his trailer, he won't have a place to live. You will in effect render the poor man homeless. You don't want that on your conscience, do you?''

''Can't have a conscience in this line of work. Interferes with business.''

''Right. Is there anything I could do?'' She didn't have much cash on her but wasn't above offering the man a bribe.

He walked around the trailer, yanking off loose pieces of metal that would raise sparks dragging on the highway. ''Drive him to a homeless shelter.''

She had to do more than that. It was her fault this was happening. Tow-Truck Early had been summoned as a direct result of her justifiably righteous indignation. He might not be the sharpest tool in the shed, but surely he could understand there was a good reason not to take the trailer.

Joe simply could not continue to stay with her. He'd changed. Instead of an easy-to-ignore redneck who told off-color jokes, he'd suddenly become sexy and polite and now talked like Gary Cooper in *High Noon*. All those spooky changes were making her crazy.

Definitely more information than Early should have to deal with.

''Lightning, you say?'' He shifted the bulging wad of chewing tobacco from one cheek to the other. ''I heard folks around town talking about that.''

''I'd consider it a big favor if you'd just leave the trailer. I'll call the mayor and straighten things out. What do you say?''

He removed his sweat-stained baseball cap and wiped his forehead with the back of his hand. ''Did the lightning singe his hair? I've heard that happens sometimes.''

''No. He was spared the indignity of hair singeing.''

''But his zipper melted, right? A guy I knew once said his uncle's zipper melted right into him. Hurt like a sonuvagun.''

''I don't know.'' Sheesh. Singed eyebrows and melted zippers were the least of Joe's problems. "So, Early, are you willing to reconsider?"

He climbed into the truck. "Nope. I got an impound order." He started the engine and headed down the drive, Joe's pitiful hovel bouncing at the end of its tether. The worthless dogs chased it all the way to the road. When it disappeared from view, they ran back and leaped around her as though seeking appreciation for their defensive efforts.

"Morons!" She kicked at a dirt clod in frustration. The quivering jumble of dog flesh slunk away, their beady eyes reproaching her lack of gratitude. "I know you all share a single brain. What I want to know is who was using it today? You're supposed to chase intruders away *before* they take your owner's stuff."

"What happened?"

Mallory spun around at the sound of Joe's voice. He must have heard the racket and limped over from the house, but was too late to retrieve his possessions. Why hadn't she rescued his stuff instead of wasting her time with the stubborn driver? She raked an errant curl out of her eyes. "Well, from the looks of things, you're officially homeless."

He looked around. "Where's the trailer?"

"On its way to R & W Salvage if my new friend Early is to be believed." Her gaze swept around the littered lot, and she couldn't help noticing how much better things looked without the trash can on wheels. When she noticed a crumpled piece of blue paper lying on the ground near the trailer's step, she scooped it up and smoothed the wrinkles. After reading it she rounded on Joe, angrier than ever. "Well, surprise, surprise! Why didn't you tell me about the notice?"

"The what?"

"You had fair warning this was going to happen."

"I did?"

"Yes." She thrust the paper under his nose. "You received the order over a week ago."

"What order?"

"The one commanding you to clean up the place by noon

today or else. You irresponsibly ignored the city's order, and losing your home is the else!''

''All that because I didn't clean house?'' He looked genuinely confused. Didn't he understand what this meant? She couldn't send him packing at the end of the week because he had no place to be packed off *to*. There was no point trying to negotiate the trailer's release from impound. It was a piece of crap and unfit for human habitation.

''No! All that because of this!'' She spun around, waving her hands to take in Joe's little Carnival of Rust. ''Maybe you don't mind living like a badger in a cootie den, but *this* is a public health hazard. What's the matter with you, Joe? What happened to make you lose what little pride you once had? Sheesh, I give up!'' She stomped away, this time down the rutted drive to the road. She'd done her bit for Mother Nature, scattering enough seedpods to reweed the Texas Panhandle.

''Wait! Mallory, slow down. Give me a chance to make this right.''

Feeling guilty for forcing him to hobble down the bumpy track on his crutches, she stopped. She'd never felt a shred of sympathy for Joe Mitchum. The opposite of a self-made man, he was self-ruined. He couldn't blame the sorry state of his affairs on anyone. So why did the unnaturally sincere note of pleading in his voice make her regret all the trouble she'd caused him?

''Mallory, I'm sorry.'' Finally catching up to her, he reached out and touched her arm. The contact set off an unlikely chain of sensations that started on her skin and quivered their way into every secret recess of her body. Her response shocked her. As did the sudden, unmistakable fragrance of roses that inexplicably filled her senses. She pulled away and looked around. Where was that scent coming from? There wasn't a rosebush for five miles in either direction.

''Do you smell that?''

''What?''

''Roses. I smell roses where there are none. Phantom flowers. I'm losing my mind. You are driving me insane!''

"I'm sorry, Mallory. I never wanted to cause trouble. But I'll make it all up to you if you'll give me another chance."

"Another chance?" She struggled to stay in hot temper mode, but all she felt was tired and defeated and...scared. "What about the chances you've thrown away over the years? Teachers saw something in you. More than one tried to help you. But you always had a natural gift for screwing up."

"I know I made mistakes—"

"Mistakes? You call what you've done mistakes? A mistake is forgetting to put fabric softener in the rinse cycle. Or buying D batteries when you need Cs. What you've done falls into the grave error category."

"I don't know what to say."

"No need to say anything. I'm not finished yet." She'd regret this later, but there was no way she could stop now. The urge to make him accept responsibility for the heartbreak he'd caused was too powerful.

He hung his head. "I'm listening."

"How many times did your mother bail you out, take you in, pay your debts? You thanked her by taking more than she could afford to give. When she got sick and lost her house, didn't she give you another chance? A chance to visit her once a week in the nursing home, sit by her bed and hold her hand before she died?"

"Mallory—"

"You've needed to hear this for a long time, and I'm gonna say it."

"You're right. I do need to hear what you have to say. Give me both barrels." His dark eyes were unmistakably wounded. Did he feel guilty? Remorseful? Ashamed? Probably not. You had to have a conscience for that.

She resumed her tirade before she ran out of steam. "You asked me for another chance. How many do you think you're entitled to? You won't hold a job. You've hurt everyone who's ever tried to befriend you. For some reason, people keep forgiving you, but you seem dedicated to underachievement. What about Brandy? That girl worked her butt off because you were unwilling to support your own family. How many times did she take you back when you cheated on her?"

"I'm sorry. I didn't know—"

"Want to know what your biggest crime is? Chloe. How many chances should you get to be the father she deserves? Yeah. I'm sorry, too, Joe. You've run out of chances as far as I'm concerned."

Will suffered Mallory's stinging words like a swarm of angry yellow jackets. He didn't try to stop her. He listened because every shortcoming she revealed was another clue in the puzzle that was Joe Mitchum. Three days in this new mortal coil had convinced him the man was a chronic no-gooder, and not worth a bucket of hot spit.

Fate had a wicked sense of humor. In an ironic twist, the unreasonably detained warrior spirit of honorable Will Pendleton now inhabited the body of a man he would have despised in every life he'd ever lived. As far as he knew, Joe wasn't a lawbreaker, but he was no model citizen either.

In his line of work, he had squeaked through some rough fixes. He'd survived ambushes and bullet hails, rockslides and flash floods. He'd looked down the muzzles of outlaws' guns and into the maws of starving wolves. But he'd never been as scared as he was right now. It wasn't just his life at stake here…it was his destiny. His eternity. He felt it slipping away, beyond his reach. Out of his control.

He'd rather face a gang of armed killers than see that disappointed look in Mallory's eyes again. Knowing he'd put it there was more than he could bear. He didn't blame her for giving up on him. Joe had let her down. Joe had let a lot of people down. He had developed a habit of hurt.

Maybe he didn't deserve another chance.

A single tear slid down Mallory's cheek. He wanted to wipe it away, hold and comfort her. Make promises. Then keep them. He wanted to love her as he had throughout time. As Molly. Before Molly. Then he saw the pain in her eyes. It was too soon for her. He'd been waiting a hundred years for this moment, but her memory had been cleared. All he was to her was the sum of Joe.

It would take a heap of good to outweigh the bad.

She expected a reply, but all he could think about was the TNT she'd exploded on him. He'd been married to a hard-working woman and had betrayed his wedding vows. He'd consorted with fast women and kept bad company. He'd failed his child. Learning Joe was a father had been the hardest pill to swallow. It was one thing to make yourself miserable, but there was a special justice reserved for people who hurt children.

Mallory started walking to the house but kept her pace slow. He tucked the clumsy crutches under his arms and matched her stride. "Please don't hate me, Mallory. I've got a lot to do, a lot to make up for. I'd sure like to think you're on my side."

"I'm not mad. I'm…disappointed and confused. You had potential, Joe. Everyone saw it. When I was in third grade, and you were in fifth, I had a terrible crush on you."

"You did?"

She rolled her eyes. "Never thought I'd admit it, but yes. You were the smartest boy at Sam Houston Elementary School. What are you going to do? Do you have any money?"

"Not much." A search of Joe's worn wallet had netted forty-seven dollars, a couple of scribbled telephone numbers, a paper car title and a French letter. "I can get a job."

"You can't work yet. You can't even walk. It'll be weeks before you can do manual labor, and you're not trained to do anything else."

"I wouldn't blame you if you tossed me out with the slop."

"I'm not an ogre." She sighed. "I won't kick you out. But I expect you to get a plan. If you're really ready to straighten up and fly right…well, I guess you can stay with me for a while longer."

"You mean that? Thank you, Mallory." No one could give him another chance. But he could make one for himself. The old Joe had done a bang-up job ruining his life, but that was before Will Pendleton climbed into the saddle. A warrior didn't back down just because the cause was lost.

"You don't owe me anything," she said softly. "Except to keep your promise this time."

"I will. You hide and watch."

Mallory steeled herself. His gratitude seemed so heartfelt she could almost believe it. She wanted to trust him, but past experience made her wary. She wouldn't be the first person to fall for Joe Mitchum's incredibly facile line of bull. He was a talented eye-wool puller. It wasn't a question of whether he could change. The big question was *would* he? He hadn't made a single good choice in his whole wasted life. Would a near-death experience be motivating enough?

"I still have work to do." She stalked off, headed for the clinic. "I'll be home in an hour or so."

"Mallory?"

"What?" She stopped but didn't turn around. She couldn't look at him. Couldn't risk having him touch her again. She was still reeling from the way she'd responded to his hand on her arm. The mysterious scent of roses coming from nowhere had totally freaked her out. She needed the normalcy of the clinic to put things in perspective. At work, she battled familiar adversaries she could understand. Like viruses and hypertension and HMOs.

"Thank you." He put a world of feeling into those two little words.

"You're welcome."

"Is there anything I can do to make things better?"

She shivered in the hot afternoon sun. When had the mere sound of his quiet, persuasive voice acquired the ability to initiate tiny electrical storms of its own? "Yeah, there is something you can do."

"Just say the word."

"Don't make me sorry I gave you another chance."

Chapter Five

For the next week, Mallory did her best to stay out of Joe's way. Which took serious effort, considering he lived in her back bedroom and poked around the house like a curiously polite building inspector. She tried to recover his trailer, but by the time she finally worked her way through the municipal food chain, it had been condemned and reduced to scrap metal, the money applied toward Joe's accumulated fines. His personal belongings had been removed before the trailer was scrapped, and the salvage yard receptionist informed him he could pick them up anytime.

Mallory contacted a few of his so-called friends, hoping someone would offer to put him up for a while. After two colorfully worded refusals and a terse hang-up, she resigned herself to playing reluctant hostess until he recovered enough to fend for himself. It wasn't that she really minded him staying with her. He was a perfect gentleman and no trouble at all. The problem was, he wasn't supposed to *be* a gentleman, and trouble had long been his middle name. She'd ragged on him to clean up his act since returning to Slapdown. Now that he'd finally taken her advice, she had no clue how to deal with him.

She had put in longer hours than usual at the clinic. Not because she was behind in her paperwork—she was too efficient to let that happen—but because she felt uneasy in Joe's newly reformed company. She continued to research lightning strike survivors in an attempt to understand Joe's transformation. In a true ah-ha moment, she finally found evidence in an obscure lightning physics journal that lent credence to a tentative hypothesis.

According to the case histories, an alcoholic petty thief had survived a lightning side flash to become a temperate and dedicated champion of the homeless. In another case, an eighteen-year-old meth-making dropout had been struck while trying to break into a pharmacy. Good prison behavior led to a reduced sentence and a year later, he'd turned his life around and was currently working his way through automotive body repair school.

When interviewed, both said they believed their survival had given them a second chance, and they felt compelled to make the most of it. While a rehabilitative bolt from the blue might be a good way for the Big Guy to get a sinner's attention, a karmic wake-up call didn't exactly fit into Mallory's scientific mindset.

The clinic had been closed a couple of hours when she finally completed notes in the last patient chart of the week. Stretching the cramps out of her writing hand, she carried the folder to the medical records area where Jeannie would file it on Monday morning. After flipping through the mail and messages in her box, she scanned next week's appointments, straightened a stack of magazines in the waiting room and returned a stray puzzle piece to the children's play table. Glancing at the clock, she realized she'd managed to stall until 8:00 p.m.

The sun would be setting soon. While she'd been busy postponing the inevitable, the rhythm of the day had changed, slowed. The workweek was over. She should go home.

Joe was waiting for her.

The unbidden thought came too readily and felt too right. It couldn't be a product of her imagination, so where had the notion come from? Tossing her lab coat in the utility caddy on the way out, she punched in the building's security code and stepped outside. The temperature had finally cooled a bit. West Texans didn't gauge the heat index on Fahrenheit or Celsius, but by whether or not an egg would fry on the sidewalk. Anything less than sunny-side up was considered balmy.

She gazed at the house on top of the hill. Heat shimmered in the air, and locusts chirruped in the grass. The setting sun smudged the dusty landscape with a golden haze, softening its harshness. Behind the house, fireflies gathered in the shadows under the scrub oaks. Not many people considered this little nowhere corner of the world beautiful, but Mallory did. She'd always loved Slapdown, had never wanted to live anywhere else. She'd grown up here, but her ties went deeper than that. Stronger than they had a reason to be, they bound her firmly to the place of her birth.

As she watched, Joe stepped out on the deck and whistled for the dogs. They came running, falling all over themselves in their haste. He poured dog chow from the twenty-five-pound bag she'd retrieved from his trailer the day after the accident. Jockeying for position around the feeding dishes, the beasts nearly knocked him off his feet, but he didn't seem to mind. His easy laughter drifted down on the soft evening breeze, touching her like a caress that made her skin prickle in response. Impossibly familiar and strangely welcome, the sound filled her with a curious mix of emotions.

Wistful homesickness and bittersweet pleasure.

It's been so long.

Dismayed, she tossed her head as if to shake the unwanted thought from her mind. Too long? Too much lukewarm Colombian blend was more like it. And a lunch consisting of two mini chocolate bars and a handful of stale peanuts. As a stressed-out intern, she'd experienced some of the more colorful symptoms of fluctuating blood sugar levels.

Mallory set the timer at the outdoor spigot behind the building. Despite the heat, she kept the grass lush and green by regularly turning on the whirling sprinklers. Without life-giving water, the lawn would go as dormant and brown as her feelings had been before Joe brought unexpected excitement into her life.

Walking up the hill, she noticed he was no longer using the crutches. When had he started getting around without them? His limp wasn't nearly as pronounced as it had been the last time she'd dared to look at him. But then she'd worked hard not to look too closely. Contact compounded the weirdness. She couldn't explain the haunting scent of nonexistent roses or elusive memories that felt like half-forgotten dreams. She wasn't into the woo-woo factor, and so had chosen distance and professional objectivity. That made it easier to believe in a logical, medically based explanation for the changes Joe seemed to have undergone since his accident.

The impossible feelings those changes had aroused in her? She was still working on those.

After sharing her home with him for a week, she'd just about ruled out brain damage. Blind spots in his long and short-term memory, as well as difficulty with words were more likely an effect of powerful pulses of electromagnetic charges. She was particularly fond of that theory because it also explained why he was acting so un-Joelike.

After all, wasn't effecting personality change the basic rationale behind electroconvulsive therapy? Shock treatments charged a severely depressed or manic patient's brain with electrical impulses in the hopes of changing his behavior. Was it such a stretch to believe the shock Joe had received might have had a positive effect on his personality?

It wasn't like he'd always been totally lacking in work ethics, personal hygiene and self-respect. He came from proud stock. Before he had so artfully tarnished it, the Mitchum name had stood for something in Slapdown. His parents had been good people, and though as poor as most families in the community, they had given their son all the advantages they could afford.

Called Little Joe because his father had been Big Joe, he'd been above-average adorable as a child. As an adolescent, he'd been bright with promise. He'd charmed his way out of the numerous scrapes he'd gotten into because it was impossible not to be snowed by his good looks, glib tongue and infectious grin. Mallory's mother claimed Joe's parents had spoiled him because he'd been the only child of their middle age. They'd never expected to have children, so they gave their son too much, stood between him and the consequences of his reckless behavior too often.

Impulsive and imprudent, Joe had gone off the deep end when his father died. A high school sophomore at the time, Mallory hadn't understood why his grief had turned into anger and then alienation. He'd lost interest in school and had dropped out. Then he seemed to lose interest in life as he was sucked into the downward spiral he'd created, each bad choice and mistake compounding the ones before.

Mallory's dad had called it the domino effect.

Up on the hill, he finished his task and leaned against the deck railing. When he turned his face up to the sky, light from the dying sun fell upon it, infusing his features with a luminosity so pure and golden, he looked like an angel come to earth. An angel? Joe Mitchum? Now there was one for the oxymoron book. Dismissing the latest of her foolish notions as one more manifestation of hypoglycemia, Mallory walked the rest of the way to the house.

Joe waved when he saw her, and his face creased in a welcoming grin. Waving back, she became aware of yet another change. All her life she'd been alone even when surrounded by people. Solitude had never bothered her, so it felt strange to think someone might be glad to see her at the end of a long day. Stranger still that she was glad to see him.

The only thing wrong with that picture was that it was Joe Mitchum. A total credibility buster. Still, what if she was right? What if the lightning hadn't changed him as much as it had simply made him forget the level to which he'd sunk in recent years? Maybe he was becoming the Joe he would have been if his world hadn't fallen apart twelve years ago.

Dicey reasoning? Maybe. But that was her theory, and she was sticking to it. The possibility that he'd been shocked into sensibility was much easier to live with than the alien pod-person explanation.

"I see you ditched the crutches." She stepped onto the deck, dodging the dogs' gosh-lady-where-you-been-all-day sniffs of greeting.

"I don't need them now. I can get around on my own two feet."

"I'll check your dressings later, and if the burns have healed adequately you can remove them, too."

"I'd like that." He held the door for her. "I'm ready to wear boots instead of limping around like a sock-footed baby."

Barefoot he might be, but he was no baby. She saw infants every day in her practice and none had ever made her heart beat faster.

Stepping inside, she was greeted by the delicious scent of cooking meat and vegetables. He followed her into the kitchen and washed his hands at the sink. He picked up a spoon and stirred the contents of a big pot.

"What are you doing?"

He looked up and smiled. "You were working so late, I figured you'd be tired and hungry when you got home. I hope you don't mind me cooking you a bite of supper."

"No, I don't mind. I told you to make yourself at home." An odd feeling washed over her. Joe had never cooked for her before; he'd never even been inside her house prior to last week. So why did the sight of him at the stove fill her with a disturbing sense of déjà vu? Just what she needed: another reason to be confused. Her rumbling stomach reminded her how long it had been since breakfast. "Smells good, whatever it is."

"Beef stew." He dipped a ladle into the simmering pot and scooped up the rich, dark gravy. He blew on it briefly and held it out, an invitation to sample his wares. "What do you think? More salt?"

She took a hesitant step, then another, her gaze lingering on his sculpted lips. Smoothly sensual, they were drawn up in an expectant smile. She wanted a taste all right, but stew was the farthest thing from her mind.

Yikes! Needing to get a grip on something, she reached for

the spoon. Joe lifted it to her mouth, and his hand brushed hers in the process. Lazy warmth curled through her, settling in her hot cheeks. "Delicious. Perfect."

She licked her lips because his were off limits. Hungrier than ever, she stepped back before she could act on the wayward impulse to push him against the counter and kiss him silly.

"It'll be ready in a minute if you want to wash up."

"I'd like to change clothes." While she was at it, she'd splash a little cold water on her face and slap some sense into herself. "I'll be right back." She glanced around the kitchen as she hurried out, half expecting a mess like she'd found in his trailer. Everything was tidy. Too tidy.

Joe dished the stew into bowls while waiting for Mallory. She returned after changing from work pants into a pair of short britches. Women wearing trousers was hard enough to get used to, but when those trousers barely covered their bare thighs...well, it never ceased to surprise him. Of course he'd watched enough television to know Mallory's denim pants and sleeveless shirt were considered modest by today's standards, but he still had to work extra hard to keep from staring at her long, shapely legs. She ran around barefoot at home and even wore paint on her toenails; two things respectable women hadn't done in his day.

Not that he minded. He never tired of looking at her, and a person couldn't get more respectable than Dr. Mallory Peterson. She'd been dodging him all week, making excuses to spend time at the clinic or in her room—anywhere but with him. He wasn't sure if she was avoiding him because she disliked him so much...or because she was finding out she didn't dislike him nearly enough.

Either way, the fact that they hadn't spent much time together or talked about anything of substance had given him plenty of time to think and work out a plan of action. He needed to save money for a place of his own, and he had the hospital bill to pay. As messed up as Joe's life had been, there was no telling what other obligations he'd have to make good on.

"You didn't have to do this, you know." She found a box of saltines in the cupboard and set it on the table, then poured cold tea into two glasses of ice. Another modern invention he never wanted to do without—the automatic icemaker.

"I wanted to show you my appreciation. It's not much, but a hot meal at the end of a long day, especially if someone else cooks it, can restore body and spirit."

"I never thought of it that way."

"You're too set on doing everything for yourself." He turned off the burner under the pot. "There's nothing wrong with letting others do for you once in awhile."

"I never had a reason to, I guess."

"You never trusted anyone enough to take care of you."

"I can take care of myself."

"Set in your ways."

"I don't think so."

"Hard-headed, then?"

"No! I'm just…independent."

"Is that what you call it?" Before she could respond, he pulled out her chair, and sat across from her. After giving thanks for the food, he picked up his spoon. "I've been thinking."

"Always an admirable pursuit. What about?"

"I believe I'm ready to go to town."

"Really? All right. No reason why you shouldn't. Where's your Jeep? It just occurred to me that it hasn't been at your place."

"My Jeep?" Not only did he not know where it was, he didn't know *what* it was.

She cocked one brow. "You don't remember where you left it?"

He started to say it had been in the towed-away trailer when she spoke again, giving him a clue. "We can figure that out later. For now, you can borrow my truck, if you want."

So a Jeep was some kind of vehicle. He wasn't sure he trusted himself driving anything that went faster than twenty miles an hour. If Celestian was right, there was a good chance Joe's skills would kick in, and he'd do fine. There was an equal chance he'd end up in the ditch. "I don't feel quite up to driving yet. I'd appreciate it if you'd take me to town."

"Sure, I can do that. Tomorrow's Saturday, we can go in the morning. We should pick up your stuff at the salvage yard anyway. Is there anything else you need?"

"I just want to look around. Check on some things. See a few people." If he wanted to start pulling his load, he needed to find out what kinds of jobs were available in the area. He didn't know what Joe's line of work had been, so he'd have to play it as it came.

As risky as it was to venture beyond the safety of Mallory's home, he needed to start living his new life instead of hiding from it. He would have to confront people he didn't recognize and couldn't know, deal with situations he might not feel up to handling. Maybe even arouse suspicions as to his true identity. It was a chance he had to take. Mallory said he needed a plan, and he'd been working on one all week. He couldn't start the wheels turning if he stayed caved up here.

"I understand." Her smile faded as she shredded a piece of beef with the side of her spoon. "Of course you want to see 'people.' I'm sure Glorieta misses you."

He nearly choked on his food. "I don't want to see *her*. It's just that—"

"You've got cabin fever."

"Well, no, I—"

"Shall I drop you off at Whiskey Pete's? That's where you and Glorieta hang out, isn't it?"

"I don't know anything about that, but—"

"You never were much of a homebody." Her look challenged him to disagree.

"Well, I always wanted to settle down. I never really had a place to call my own." Not until he'd bought the little house at the edge of town, the one with a cottonwood tree in the yard and a threshold he could carry his bride over. A bride whose face grew a little dimmer each day. A bride who had started to resemble Mallory in his memories.

The three-room clapboard house had felt like a palace to him after living in the saddle for so many years. It even had a porch, and the other Rangers had poked fun at him, saying they couldn't believe he was trading his horse for a rocking chair. They'd been his *compadres* for years, yet he couldn't remember their names. Even their faces had faded like worn photographs. Celestian had warned him that in time he'd lose the details of his life as Will Pendleton. He hadn't thought he'd lose so much so soon.

He recalled how he'd laughed off the other Rangers' joshing, claiming they were envious of his good fortune. He'd looked forward to being a family man.

"This is really tasty. I'm impressed." Mallory ate hungrily, and he refilled her bowl before she could ask for seconds. "I had no idea you could cook."

He shrugged. "I suspect there's a lot about me you don't know."

Her spoon stopped halfway to her mouth. "Yes. I think you might be right about that."

He ate his own supper but felt her watching him. "What's wrong?"

"I just noticed that you are in sore need of a trim."

He brushed his overgrown hair back from his forehead. "I couldn't find the scissors and kept forgetting to ask where you keep them."

"I'll cut it for you."

"You'd do that?"

She seemed alarmed by the offer. "Sure. Why not?"

The day before the first lightning bolt had felled him, he'd sat in Molly's front yard in a straight-back chair with a towel around his shoulders. He'd told her he could do it himself, but she'd insisted. The wedding was only a few days away, and she wanted him to look his best for their portrait. He'd nearly come unwrapped, overwhelmed by the languid feel of her hands in his hair, the intoxicating scent of the rosewater she wore, and the merry sound of her chatter as she discussed their future.

He was poised to take the biggest step of his life, but all he could think about was bedding Molly Earnshaw. Once the parson sanctioned their union, he planned to make love to her until time lost its meaning and he forgot where he left off and she began.

He grinned. "I think we should do it outside."

Her eyes widened. "Oh, right. Haircut. We'll have to hurry before it gets too dark."

"Some things you shouldn't ought to rush through." He captured her gaze, unsure if they were still talking about the same thing.

"Like haircuts?" she asked with a smile.

"Yeah, those too."

After stacking their bowls in the sink and wiping the counter, Mallory located the scissors. What *had* she been thinking when she volunteered to trim Joe's hair? That was the problem. She wasn't thinking these days. For some reason when she was around him, things just popped into her head or blurted out of her mouth. She couldn't believe she was going to do this when she'd vowed to keep her distance.

Joe was sitting on one of the patio chairs. Waiting. She took a deep breath and stepped out onto the deck. "So. How do you want me to cut it?"

He shrugged. As Will, he'd worn his hair short, but Joe seemed to prefer his longer. "Whatever you think."

"Maybe a little off the top? Even up the sides and back?"

"Sounds good. I should wear a towel to keep the hair off my shirt."

"Or you can just take your shirt off." She had to keep her mouth shut around him because she couldn't seem to control what would come out of it next. While she was still dealing with the mental image of a bare-chested Joe, the real thing materialized. He slipped his black T-shirt over his head and draped it over the deck railing.

No problem. She just wouldn't look. It wasn't the hair on his chest she had to touch.

"Anything wrong?" He turned and looked up at her.

"No. What could possibly be wrong?"

"I don't know. But you haven't started yet."

"I was…deciding on a style." For Pete's sakes, why didn't

she just get on with it? She'd done far more serious cutting in her medical career. Trimming a little hair was nothing compared to the cadaver lab. "Okay. Here goes."

The second she touched him, a tingling sensation wiggled its way up her fingers, through her hand and arm, then spread over her body. This was ridiculous. It was just hair. So why did it smell like roses? She leaned down and sniffed as unobtrusively as possible. No roses. He smelled like rain-scented soap and...the black pepper he'd shaken into his stew. She doggedly ignored the crazy feelings flitting around inside her and got busy snipping and trimming, evening out his do-it-yourself haircut.

"Dr. McKinley called me at the clinic today to check on you."

"Did he?"

"He considers you a medical miracle of sorts."

"I don't know about that."

"What *do* you know?" she asked.

"What do you mean?"

"What do you remember about...the way things were before the accident?"

"Not much. But from what you told me the other day, I must have been a ring-tailed tooter."

She laughed at his unusual choice of words. "Well, I don't know what a ring-tailed tooter is, but yeah, I'm guessing you were one."

"I feel bad about all the wrong I've done."

"That's a start. Now maybe you can do right."

"I want to. I know I can't undo all the hurt I've heaped on people, but I aim to try."

He sounded so sincere, she believed surviving the lightning strike really had been a life-changing experience for him. The fact that he also sounded like Gary Cooper's western marshal wasn't so easily explained.

"That's all anyone can do, Joe. Try." She combed through the glossy strands, trimming the ends. Considering this was the first time she'd ever cut hair, her fingers seemed to know what they were doing. It almost felt like they *remembered* how.

"I want to cut the grass for you."

"What?"

"The grass around the trailer and the clinic. Who takes care of that?"

"Different people. The townsfolk take turns. I like to garden, so I do it myself when I have time."

"I'll handle it from now on. Just show me where the grass cutter's kept."

Grass cutter, lawn mower. Same difference. "Okay." Maybe he really did want to do the right thing for a change.

"I need to work and pay my way. It doesn't feel right to take advantage of your hospitality without giving back in return."

"I appreciate that. Thanks." She laid the scissors and comb on the patio table and handed him the mirror she'd brought out. "What do you think?"

He gazed into the glass, turning first one way and then another, staring at his own image like he'd never really seen it before. "Not a bad-looking fella."

She laughed. "Now you sound like the old Joe."

"You did a good job." He stood and reached for his shirt. She reached for it at the same time, and their hands touched. Before she could pull away, he threaded his fingers through hers and brought her hand to his chest. The steady beat of his heart beneath her palm and the warmth of his skin conspired to leave her breathless. "Mallory."

"Will." She swallowed hard. "Will you let…go of me?"

"I'm not sure I can." He stepped even closer, and now she could feel the heat of his body reach out to her. "I've waited so long."

It's been so long. The same thought she'd had earlier sprang unbidden into her thoughts once more. What was happening? Joe's head lowered, and she stretched to find his questing lips. A powerful spark of longing fired through her, and he deepened the kiss, matching need with need. He tugged her onto his bare chest, and her palm cupped the muscles that tensed at her touch. Her other hand slipped over his shoulder and up his neck into his hair, seeking to increase the pressure, prolong the pleasure.

He moaned and enfolded her in his embrace. His tongue danced with hers, opening a floodgate that let a rush of longing and desire roar through her. If he weren't holding her so tightly, she would be unable to stand because her legs had inexplicably gone numb.

What was happening? She'd never felt so overwhelmed with emotion. Had never known a physical reaction could be so powerful. The earth had tilted and she was losing control. If she didn't put an end to this madness, she'd tug him down on the deck and have her way with a man who might not be in his right mind. She pushed against his chest, trying to break the molten contact of their bodies.

"Mallory, I missed you." He sighed and tipped his forehead against hers.

"Will…" The word felt right in her mouth, as familiar as a much-repeated prayer. She said it again with the same effect, before getting out the rest of the question. "Will…you stop it? We can't do this." She wrenched away from him, backing up several steps.

"I'm sorry." He took an equal number of steps toward her. "No. I'm not sorry. I've been wanting to do that for…a long time."

"Don't say that! You're just complicating everything." Her pulse pounded in her ears until she could no longer hear the chirping insects.

"Things *are* complicated!" He reached for her, but she dodged him. "I just wish I could make you understand."

"I understand this can't happen again."

"Why not? You can see how right it is."

"I can't see anything! I'm blinded by emotions that aren't even mine."

"You can't deny you felt something when we kissed."

She raked a loose curl out of her eyes. "That's the problem."

"How can what we just shared be a problem?"

Raw desire slithered through her, and Mallory's heart pounded with the realization that she wanted Joe Mitchum with every fiber of her being. "It's a problem because I feel like I've kissed you a hundred times before!"

A slow smile started at his mouth and spread into his eyes, which were as dark and mysterious as the shadows that wrapped them in intimacy. "What could possibly be wrong with that?"

"Everything! It doesn't make sense."

"Not everything is logical, Mallory."

"In my world it is. I don't know how I let this happen, but I do know it can't happen again." She left him staring after her as she ran into the house and slammed her bedroom door.

Chapter Six

On the way to town the next morning Mallory stopped by the salvage yard. Joe insisted she wait in the truck while he went in the office to fetch his things. When he came out carrying two cardboard boxes containing all his worldly possessions, his expression was solemn. She respected his silence. Did he think, as she did, that thirty years of living should have produced more than this pitiful collection? That a man should have more to show for his life?

Downtown Slapdown was Saturday-busy, buzzing with locals going about their business and tourists hunting for bargains in the thriving antique stores. Mallory dropped Joe off at the square where old men sat in the shade. He was vague about his plans, and she didn't ask for details. The less involved she was in his life, the better.

She had a few errands of her own to run, so they arranged to meet later at the diner and said goodbye. Glancing in the rearview mirror, she watched as Joe looked around in wide-eyed confusion. He walked tentatively off the curb at the corner and then jumped back as a car rounded the corner and honked. If she didn't know better, she'd swear he'd never stepped foot in his hometown before.

A stranger in a strange land. Why was she still surprised by the odd thoughts that popped into her head these days?

This morning when she'd unwrapped his dressings to examine the burns, latex gloves had saved her from touching him and thus embarrassing herself with a reaction like the one she'd had last night. She couldn't wear a biohazard suit when dealing with him, so she'd have to be extra careful. She wasn't willing to open any more doors between herself and a man who filled her with uncontrollable feelings she couldn't explain.

Long after retreating to her room, she'd lain awake trying to understand how she'd let that kiss happen. How in a split second he'd stolen her breath away. She'd known Joe most of her life. Her third grade crush had worn off by the end of the term, and she hadn't felt remotely attracted to him since. So what had happened last night?

The emotion sparking between them had been more than simple attraction. Chemistry she could deal with. She hadn't been involved with anyone in, well…forever, and it stood to reason her hormones might be a little feisty. It was possible said hormones had simply outvoted common sense. For a few minutes, the queen of control had lost it. Not normal, but hardly bizarre enough to declare martial law.

The distressing part was the undeniable sense that falling into Joe's arms had somehow been *right*. That it was inevitable. Meant to be. A kiss shouldn't feel like an out-of-body experience. Especially a *familiar* out-of-body experience. That was above and beyond the call of spooky.

Maybe she'd blown the situation all out of proportion by reading more into one kiss than she should have. After all, it had been amazing. Stir-you-down-to-your-toes passionate. Everything-you-ever-dreamed-of perfect. Too powerful to ignore, but too good to be true.

She'd settled two things by the time she'd driven to her favorite grocery store on the opposite side of town. One, no way could a couple of weeks of good behavior make her overlook twelve years of accumulated mistakes, and two, no more kissing. Since direct contact seemed to intensify her unsettling responses, she would avoid so much as a handshake in the future. Which might be hard to do while living in such close quarters.

Clearly, if she wanted to get Joe Mitchum off her mind, she had to get him out of her house.

Where could he stay? She'd already been through the short list of possibilities and had come up with zip. Nada. One guy had, however, offered to take a dog off Joe's hands. Apparently, in Slapdown, it was easier to find a home for a stray mutt than it was to secure temporary housing for a screwed-up human.

People stopped to chat and seek free medical advice as she pushed her cart up and down the aisles, so it took longer than she planned to locate the items on her list. Topics included the unseasonably hot weather, the annual 4-H bake sale and next week's immunization clinic. The retirement of longtime county sheriff, Nate Egan, was of considerable interest, as a suitable candidate to replace him had yet to step forward.

One of the charms of small-town living was the friendly people, but could she really call any of those who'd stopped to talk a friend? She recognized every face in town. Few hesitated to seek her opinion when they had a troublesome plantar's wart. Too bad no one wanted to listen to her problems. Briny Tucker came closest to being a friend, but his new life and new wife kept him pretty busy these days.

Her mother said you had to be a friend to have one, and Mallory had always been too focused on her goals to let anyone get close. A girlfriend would come in handy right now. She visited with the cashier as she checked out, but her heart wasn't in it. Feeling more alone than ever, she pushed the cart of groceries out into the sunshine.

Her mother was a good listener, but Joe wasn't a topic they could discuss. Besides, her parents were on a six-week RV vacation, camping with several other couples in Glacier National Park at the moment. If she could reach them at their campsite, what would she say? Hi, just checking in. Hope you're having a good time. Oh, by the way, don't be alarmed, but your hard-working daughter has come down with a *Twilight Zone* case of the hots for the town bum.

She'd always been a lone wolf when it came to emotions, but this thing with Joe wasn't a fix-it-yourself problem. It required the objective point of view of someone who'd been there and done that and donated the T-shirt to a worthy cause. Someone with a little more worldliness than could be readily acquired in Slapdown society.

Barring that, she'd settle for a qualified mental health professional.

She crossed the parking lot and was startled out of deep contemplation mode when she rounded a van and saw who was waiting beside her truck. Leaning against the fender like an elegant blond answer to her prayers was Dorian Burrell Tucker, wearing a tangerine Neiman-Marcus crop pantsuit that was way too glam for Sav-Mart.

Normally, Mallory didn't question divine directives such as "ask and ye shall receive," but this was definitely pushing it.

Dorian lifted her designer sunglasses and waved. "Hi, Mallory. It's good to see you again."

"Hey, stranger, what are you doing here?" She'd met the heir to the Chaco Oil fortune in college, but they hadn't traveled in the same circles until Dorian married Briny. The Tuckers split their time between their Dallas penthouse and the Burrell ranch, so Mallory hadn't seen much of them since their Christmas wedding. Because Briny was on the clinic's board of directors, she'd spoken to him on the phone about clinic business, but as far as she knew, the couple hadn't visited Slapdown since early spring. Which made it even odder that Dorian had shown up today—precisely when Mallory most needed a sympathetic feminine ear.

"Brindon had business in town. We would've called, but it came up at the last minute. I saw your truck and told him to go on, I'd wait for you." She laughed. "If you have other plans, I'm totally stranded."

"No. I don't have plans. As a matter of fact, I have a couple of hours to kill, but I need to take these groceries home." Mallory stowed the bags in the back.

"Great." Dorian buckled her seat belt and turned to Mallory with a happy smile. "We have a lot of catching up to do."

Joe looked around in wonder. Slapdown sure had changed in the past hundred years. The saplings the Daughters of the Republic had planted in the square had grown into tall oaks. His last trip through, there had been eight saloons and one church in town. Now it seemed to be the other way around. The biggest surprise, besides the flashing red and green lights at the corners, was the merchandise stocked by the stores on Main Street.

Sauntering down the sidewalk, he recognized many of the items displayed in the windows of what the signs called antique shops. Old china and rusty hand tools. Chamber pots and quilts and mantel clocks. Why would people buy such outdated things when they could have time-saving modern inventions instead?

He had no clear notion where he was going, so he moseyed around, hoping to spot a Help Wanted sign or a work boss putting together a crew. In his time, men from outlying ranches came to town on Saturdays to hire extra hands. He didn't have any experience punching cows, but he was good at gentling horses.

As he passed a garage, a man in grimy overalls rolled out from under a chunked-up automobile and flagged him down. "Joe! Hey, there, Joe Mitchum!"

"Howdy! Bob." More people should wear their names on their pockets. It sure made life easier.

"Say, buddy, you bringing me the title for the Jeep?" Bob walked toward him, wiping his hands on a greasy rag. "The check I gave you cleared the bank, so I'd like to settle up now you're back on your feet."

Title? Why did that sound familiar? Right, the folded piece of green paper he'd found in Joe's wallet. Unsure what the transaction entailed, he decided to play along, hoping Bob would let loose a few more details. "Yeah, got it right here." He extracted the paper and handed it over.

"Let's go inside. My old lady's got the truck title ready for you."

"Sounds good." Except he had no idea what he was talking about.

"I got the Wrangler running, but it would have cost you big time if you'd had to pay for fixing the transmission yourself. You made the right decision to sell it."

So Joe had sold the vehicle Mallory had mentioned. He followed Bob into a small, grimy office.

"How are you, Joe?" The dark-haired woman behind the desk had to be Mrs. Bob. "We heard you got hit by lightning."

"I'm fine now."

"You're a lucky man." She handed him a pen to sign the title.

"That I know."

Joe was amazed at the ease with which he scrawled his new name, even if the signature wasn't in his handwriting. It must have looked like the old Joe's because neither Bob nor his missus questioned him.

Bob handed him a set of keys and a different title. "I put a new clutch in the Ford. It ought to get you around for a while." The garage owner peered at him suspiciously. "You ain't thinking of backing out, are you? We agreed. Two grand and the '84 Ford truck for the Wrangler."

"No, Bob. A deal's a deal. My word is my bond."

Bob laughed. "Oh yeah? Since when?" He slapped Joe's shoulder. "The Ford's parked out back. Take it now and get it out of my way."

He didn't know how to drive, so he hoped Celestian was right, and Joe's old skills would kick in. He followed Bob through the garage to a parking lot in the rear.

"There she is. What do you think? I had Moe buff out some of those dents for you."

"Looks good. I appreciate it."

"If she gives you any trouble, let me know." Bob slapped him once more for good measure and went inside.

Joe stared at the dusty green truck. It was an ugly contraption. What made people think these fume-spewing machines were an improvement over horses? He climbed in the cab, inserted the key in the slot and turned it as he'd seen Mallory do. The engine roared to life. Placing his left hand on the steering wheel, he used his right to pull the gear lever into position.

Without conscious thought, his left foot pressed down on one of the floor pedals while his right foot eased off the middle one and pushed down the one on the right. He clipped a trash can as he backed out of the lot and sent it rolling into the street, but driving wasn't nearly as hard as he thought it would be. How could something he'd never done before seem so familiar? By the time he circled the block twice, he was confident he could manage without running down innocent folks.

Relieved that for once, Celestian had known what he was talking about, he marveled at the uncanny way his body seemed to know how to perform unknown tasks. Too bad his brain didn't understand half of what he was doing. Parking in front of the bank, he switched off the engine. Hopefully banking hadn't changed as much as transportation.

If the old Joe hadn't put Bob's check for the Jeep in the bank, he was in deep trouble. If he'd cashed it and stashed the money in the trailer it was long gone. He pushed open the heavy door and walked into the cool, dim lobby. He turned around, amazed that everything looked the same as he remembered, except for the computers.

"How can I help you?" The young lady teller had seemed friendly enough until she looked up.

"Name's Joe Mitchum, ma'am." He'd worried about stumbling over the name and was surprised at how easily it rolled off his tongue.

"Like I don't know who you are. What can I do for you?" According to the metal plate at the window, the teller's name was Doreen Briggs. Doreen didn't seem happy to see him.

Joe placed a worn bankbook on the counter. He'd found it in the back pocket of a pair of old jeans Mallory had gathered up in her swoop through the trailer. The last entry in the book had been made over six months ago, and the balance wasn't near what it should have been. "I was hoping you could tell me if I still have an account here, ma'am."

Without bothering to look at the account number, the teller typed information into the computer keyboard. "You haven't closed the account, so yes, it's still open."

He had no idea what he'd done to merit the young woman's hostility and didn't care to hazard a guess. The old Joe hadn't exactly had a winning way about him. "Can you tell me if I have a balance?"

She punched a few more keys. "The funds from your last deposit are now available." In an angry whisper, she added, "but I'm not."

"I beg your pardon?" Maybe banking *had* changed more than he thought.

"*That* particular account is closed."

"I don't understand. I thought—"

"Don't expect any more customer relations." She glared at him.

"I'm sorry, ma'am. I just want to find out—"

"Oh! Here's your stupid balance." Frowning, she scribbled a figure on a slip of paper and slid it across the counter. "Will that be all?"

He breathed a sigh of relief. The whole two thousand was there. Plus a little extra. "Can I withdraw some of this now?"

"You can withdraw it all if you want. But make up your mind, there are other customers waiting."

Despite the teller's impatience, he hesitated. It didn't feel right, taking a dead man's money. But technically he was Joe now, and since he had to live Joe's life and deal with Joe's problems, was it a crime to finance that life with Joe's savings? He'd expected things to become complicated once he left the security of Mallory's home, but this was an unexpected twist.

Doreen cleared her throat. "What'll it be, *Mr.* Mitchum?"

"I'd like to take out two hundred and fifty dollars please."

"Always the big spender," Doreen muttered loud enough for him alone to hear.

The teller's animosity disturbed him. He hoped Joe didn't have too many enemies.

His next stop was the western wear store down the block. Mallory had okayed the removal of his bandages that morning, and he was ready for some new boots. He tried on several styles until he found a serviceable pair of leathers that weren't too expensive and didn't hurt his feet. In his ranger days, good boots had been as important as a clean rifle and a sturdy mount. He couldn't wear the flimsy soft-soles Mallory called running shoes. What kind of man needed special shoes to run in?

He gazed longingly at the display of sharp-brimmed Stetsons, but the price tags convinced him a no-name hat would keep the sun off his head just as well as the real thing. He was the only customer in the store, and with the white-haired owner's help, he selected three long-sleeved western shirts, two pairs of denim pants, a big bag of thick socks and another one of skivvies.

Everything cost more now. The new wardrobe would carve a sizeable chunk out of his windfall, but clothing was a necessity. The riggin's he'd been wearing weren't fit for grease rags, and he didn't feel comfortable going around with undershirts on the outside, all of them decorated with writing promoting beer and grateful dead people. A real man took pride in his appearance. He couldn't expect others to respect him, if he didn't respect himself. Human nature being what it was, if he wanted folks to think he was a new man, he'd have to look the part.

"You're Joe Mitchum, aren't you?" The storekeeper was a stoop-shouldered man who carried the purchases to a cash register that looked like it had been built during his *last* lifetime. "The fella struck by lightning?"

"Yessir, that's me."

"I don't believe you've ever shopped in here before."

"You've got a nice store. You'll be seeing a lot of me from now on."

The man returned Joe's grin as he tallied the sale. "Will there be anything else?"

"Well, sir, I'd like to wear some of these duds out of here. Mind if I change in your little room back there?"

"Not at all." He tried not to look too curious as he directed Joe to the fitting room.

A few minutes later, Joe stepped out dressed up like a sore wrist. The salesman looked him over good this time. "If you don't mind me saying so, young fella, you look plumb different."

"Good." Joe donned his new white hat and ran his thumb along the brim. "Different is exactly what I was going for."

The storekeeper was friendlier than the bank teller, most likely because they'd had no personal dealings in the past. He extended a hand, and Joe shook it. "That was a close call you had, young fella. Lightning can put a man in the ground. Glad to have you back."

"Glad to be back." He picked up his packages. "You wouldn't know of any work to be had, would you?"

"You looking for a job?" The undisguised surprise in the man's voice told him Joe's reputation had preceded him again.

"Yessir, I sure am."

"What kind of work you interested in?"

"Whatever I can find."

The man paused. "Are you serious?"

"As serious as a snakebite."

"Well, I heard Tag Peeler was looking for laborers to frame houses. You might check with him."

"Thank you…sir, I'll do that." Not knowing people's names put a kink in the rope, one Celestian's crew should have worked out by now. Still, a man couldn't go wrong with a polite sir or ma'am.

"Just tell him Whitey White sent you."

He smiled. "Thanks again, Mr. White."

He didn't know where to find Tag Peeler's crew, but figured if he kept walking around, he'd run into someone to direct him. After dumping his purchases in the front seat of his new old truck, he smoothed the crisp front of his fresh white shirt, sloshed his hat at a jack-deuce angle and headed down the street with no clear destination in mind.

For now, it was enough to feel the sun on his face, fill his lungs with clean, hot air and listen to lively sounds made by flesh-and-blood people. Walking on feet that didn't hurt with every step and wearing real clothes instead of bum rags was pure gravy.

It was still too early to meet Mallory, but when he passed the café, he decided to stop in for a cup of coffee. A bell over the door tinkled, and heads turned in his direction. He removed his hat as his mother had taught him, and it was clear by the expressions startling around the room that folks were surprised when they recognized him. Voices lowered and quiet conversation buzzed over the sound of clattering dishes and the fan whirring overhead. No one spoke to him.

He settled on a stool at the counter and placed his hat on his lap. He sighed with relief when the middle-aged waitress approached. She was wearing her name to make his life easier, so he addressed her with a familiarity he didn't feel.

"Morning, Dot."

"Mornin', Joe. You want your regular?" She stood behind the counter with a pot of coffee in her hand.

"If my regular's a cup o' black and one of those sinkers, I do."

She filled his cup, then removed a donut from under a glass dome and placed it on a small plate in front of him. "You look in pretty good shape for somebody who caused a false alarm in Heaven."

"Never better. I heard Tag Peeler might be looking for hands. Do you know anything about that?"

"Tag's got a couple of new houses going up, so he might need help. Are you wanting work?"

"I sure am."

"I take it parting out wrecks didn't pan out like you thought?"

He wasn't sure what she meant and gave her the all-purpose male response. A shrug. "I'm looking to make a decent wage, is all."

"Well, I think Tag's gone to Odessa for his folks' anniversary party this weekend, but he'll be in bright and early Monday morning. Want me to put in a word for you?"

"Would you do that?" It was a relief to meet another person the old Joe hadn't provoked.

"Be glad to. Your mama was a friend of mine, and I told her I'd watch out for you if I could. You still staying with Doc Peterson? Want me to tell Tag to call you out there?"

"I'd be much obliged."

"Ooh, much obliged, huh?" Dot grinned. "I thought you'd been to the hospital, not to charm school."

The man on the stool beside him swiveled around. "You don't appear to be too fried around the edges."

Dot slapped at his hand. "You hush, Harmon. Don't pick on the boy." She leaned on the counter and turned to Joe. "Never mind him. But you know, you do look—"

"Different?" he supplied. At least people had noticed.

"Yeah, that too. But I was gonna say good. You look good, Joe." She poked a graying strand of hair under her cap. "If I was twenty years younger and fifty pounds lighter, I'd give you a run for your money."

"That's a mighty generous offer, Dot." He sipped the hot coffee. It was just the way he liked it. Thicker than axle grease and twice as tasty. Not like the thin-blooded, cinnamon flavored brew that Mallory served.

The man named Harmon spoke. "Tell me, Mitchum. Did you have one of them near-death experiences like on The Discovery Channel where you see the white light and hear the angels singing and all that crap?"

"No. I don't believe I did."

"I heard you died, but the doc revived you."

"Yes, that's what happened."

"Don't reckon there's a chance you glimpsed the pearly gates. I heard your feet were burned. Got too close to the fiery furnace, huh?"

"Harmon Biddle, if you don't hush up, I'm gonna break your yolks." Dot wiped the counter in front of Joe's tormentor with a rag, but made it clear she could just as easily wipe the floor with Harmon.

"Heck, Dot. I was just kidding around. I didn't mean anything." He turned to Joe. "Just giving you a hard time."

"No harm done." He dipped his donut in his cup and took a bite of the soggy pastry.

"Hey there, Joe." A feminine voice purred beside him as a soft hand slithered across his back. "How come you been such a stranger, baby?"

He looked up and the gum-chewing blonde with the butter-fly tattoo fluttered spidery lashes at him. "Glorieta."

"Lordy, Joe, you look good enough to eat. Why haven't you called me?" She shot Harmon the evil eye, and he slid down the counter. She perched on the one he vacated and crossed her legs.

"I've been busy."

"We'll have to get together. Real soon." She licked her cotton candy-pink lips.

Clearly, Joe and Glorieta had a history. So how could he get rid of her without being a bounder? He coughed. Her perfume would make a gut-wagon driver's eyes water.

Dot to the rescue. Again. "What'll it be, girl? Did you come in here to eat or just to drool on my customers?"

The blonde shot the older woman a dagger look, but it bounced off Dot's sturdy, no-nonsense veneer. "I came in to talk to *my* friend. Which I can't do if you keep butting in."

Dot harrumphed and moved away to refill Harmon's cup.

"I'm going to Whiskey Pete's tonight. The Sagebrush Brotherhood's playing, and you still owe me a dance." Glorieta giggled and leaned into him, rubbing the inside of his leg with fingers capped with long, scary-looking pink nails.

Joe detected the stale odor of tobacco under the perfume. When he didn't respond, she went on. "Remember last time? We were going to do the Electric Glide, but we got a little sidetracked in the parking lot."

Dot slung the counter rag over her shoulder and squared off with Glorieta. "Oh, I forgot to tell you, hon. Warren Pickens was in here earlier looking for you."

Glorieta turned to the waitress with an annoyed huff. "Oh, yeah? What'd that fool want?"

"He said to tell you he got his lab results back and you two need to talk."

Glorieta's heavily made-up eyes narrowed. "Thanks for the update, Granny." She placed her hand on Joe's shoulder. "Will I see you tonight, honey?"

Not if he saw her first. His shrug must have irritated her because she shot him a killing look. To his overwhelming relief, she wiggled off the stool and out the door.

Joe finished his coffee. "How much do I owe you, Dot?"

"Buck fifty. No extra charge for the leech removal."

He placed three dollars on the counter. "Thanks for watching my back. You'd be a good one to ride the river with."

"You be careful out there, honey. Beware of scavengers." She winked. "You know, coyotes, vultures and predatory blondes."

Stepping outside, Joe blinked in the bright sunlight. Walking back to his truck, he heard someone call out to him. A big shiny black automobile that didn't look like a car or a truck but a combination of the two pulled up to the curb.

"Hey, Joe! I almost didn't recognize you." A well-dressed man about his own age climbed out, and before Joe could respond, he was wrapped in a powerful bear hug. The man stepped back, his gaze raking Joe from the top of his new hat to the tip of his new boots. "You're looking good, buddy."

"I feel good." With no name embroidered on the man's expensive-looking shirt, Joe didn't have a clue who his admirer might be.

"I wanted to come and see you before, but I couldn't get away until now. Mallory told me what happened to your trailer. Sorry to hear about that."

"It needed to happen."

"Mal felt bad about it, though. She didn't know her complaint would cause so much trouble."

Joe smiled. So Mallory was the one who'd alerted the town council to the mess next door. Good for her. "She was just being a good citizen."

"Glad there's no hard feelings." The man slapped him on the back. "I wasn't sure what kind of shape you'd be in after being zapped off a pole, but I have to say, you look like a new man!" He swatted Joe's arm in a brotherly way. "I had no idea a little do-it-yourself-shock treatment could have such a positive effect on a person."

"I guess you could say I've seen the light. I mean to get myself straightened out."

"That's good because I'm here to help you."

Recognition finally dawned on Joe. The man was Brindon Tucker, the fella who'd won all the millions in some kind of lottery. Mallory had talked about him often enough, and had shown Joe a picture of him and his beautiful new bride.

Based on the surprisingly positive reception he'd received, Tucker wasn't just Mallory's friend he was also Joe's. Lord knew he needed one of those.

Chapter Seven

Mallory was glad she had groceries to take home. She wanted to discuss Joe with Dorian, but could hardly do so in any of Slapdown's public places. Friendly was fine, but some of the locals were known to express a little too much interest in other people's business. A few were front-line competitors in the triathlon of eavesdropping, gossiping and rumormongering.

The women caught up on each other's activities on the drive out to the house. After storing the food in her cheerful yellow kitchen, Mallory offered to make ice tea, and they talked at the table while waiting for the water to boil.

Mallory gave Dorian an assessing look. "Judging by your goofy grin of complete and utter satisfaction, I'm guessing married life agrees with you."

"It's wonderful." Dorian's heartfelt sigh reminded Mallory of what was missing in her own life. "Brindon is absolutely the best thing that ever happened to me."

"I guess it's just a coincidence that he says the same thing about you."

"He's such a sweetheart. If I'd known being married to him

would be so wonderful, I would have said yes the first time he asked.''

"Wouldn't that have taken some of the fun out of the pursuit?" Mallory teased.

"Being pursued is all right," Dorian admitted with a sly twinkle in her eye. "But being caught is *way* better."

They shared a laugh as Mallory poured hot water over the tea bags. "Winning the lottery and becoming an instant millionaire had to be a big adjustment for Briny. I give you credit for helping him adapt so quickly."

"He's taught me much more than I could ever teach him." Solemn and sincere, Dorian's words convinced Mallory the couple was as happy as they seemed.

"Does he like the new job?" With her chic clothes and salon hair, Dorian looked like a page from *Town and Country*. It was pointless to compare herself to the socialite, but Mallory couldn't help feeling a little too plain and country in her simple print sundress.

"He was hesitant when my grandmother first suggested he take over Chaco Oil. I had to convince him all those years working on the rigs gave him the background he needed to become an excellent CEO. The employees love him, and he's really taking to management."

"And is your grandmother taking to retirement?"

"As usual Prudence Burrell is a piece of work." Dorian laughed. "She's spending the summer at a chalet in Switzerland with a guy named Gustav."

"What about you? What are you doing these days?" Besides looking perfect and making Briny happy.

"I'm overseeing the Marion Tucker Foundation. Brindon put most of the proceeds from the lottery into a charitable endowment, which he named after his late mother. I help administer the funds."

"The work must agree with you." Mallory eyed her approvingly. "You're positively glowing."

Dorian blushed. "You know, I've been getting that a lot lately."

"As a physician, I feel qualified to venture a differential diagnosis."

"I can save you the trouble." The blonde's face lit up with joy. "Brindon and I are expecting a baby in January. But don't tell anyone yet. We aren't ready to announce."

"Your secret's safe with me. Congratulations." Mallory arranged cookies on a small plate and set it in the center of the table, then filled two glasses with ice cubes and poured the tea. "Lemon?"

"Please. Is it decaffeinated? I'm supposed to avoid caffeine."

"It's ginger peach herbal. No caffeine." She set the glasses on the table. "Briny must be thrilled about the baby."

"He's beyond thrilled. Because his own father ran out on him when he was a kid, he's determined to be the best dad in the world."

"He will be. He's a great guy who deserves all the good things that have happened to him." Despite the fact that she'd been away for years completing her education, Mallory considered Briny the brother she'd never had. They'd kept in touch, and he'd been instrumental in making her dream of a clinic for Slapdown reality.

Sunshine slanted through the window and pooled on the table, reminding Mallory how bright Brindon and Dorian's world was. They had it all. Youth, beauty, wealth, love and now a baby on the way. She didn't want to envy them, but their happiness tugged at her heart. Even though she'd wanted to be a doctor for as long as she could remember, work just hadn't been enough to fill the loneliness in her life lately. "I'm truly happy everything's working out so well for both of you."

"Thanks, Mallory. I'm lucky to have you for a friend." Dorian sipped her tea and smiled. "Enough about the Tuckers. What's up with Joe Mitchum?"

"What have you heard?" Mallory kept her tone casual.

"Just the basics. He was struck by lightning, and you saved him."

Mallory nodded. "The actual saving part was a bit more complicated, but that'll work for *Readers Digest*." As much as she needed another opinion, she wasn't ready to jump in and tell Dorian about all the strange things that had happened lately.

"Brindon told me about the trailer and how Joe's been living with you."

Mallory leaned back in her chair. "The arrangement was supposed to be temporary, but I couldn't find anyone else willing to take him in."

Dorian leaned forward on her folded arms. "This is going to sound harsh, but I'll tell you the same thing I tell Brindon. There are some people on whom kindness is wasted. They live in a bottomless pit of need. No matter what you do for them, it's never enough to pull them out of the messes they make. Helping them only reinforces their dependence."

"I know." Mallory sighed. Dorian didn't know how Joe had changed. "I agree in theory. But if I hadn't helped him, I would have wasted a lot of time on guilt."

Dorian reached out and patted Mallory's arm. "It's not your fault Joe Mitchum is homeless."

"Actually, it is." Mallory wished guilt was all there was to her feelings for Joe. It would make everything so much easier.

"If you hadn't reported him, someone else would have. He had a perfectly good chance to clean up his act, and he chose not to."

"I know, but—"

"No buts. Black hole of need, remember? As any lifeguard can tell you, if you're not careful the person you're trying to save can drown you, too." Dorian helped herself to a cookie. "I've always wondered why Brindon thinks so much of Joe. He just says they go back a long way."

"Briny sees something in Joe the rest of us don't." Brindon Tucker's kindness and generosity had been legendary long before he lucked out in the lottery. Even as a poor oil rigger, he'd been everyone's best friend. But he'd had a particular fondness for Joe Mitchum.

"I can't complain if Brindon's worst character flaw is seeing the best in people." Dorian obviously thought her new husband was pretty perfect. "From what I've heard about Joe, friendship with him can be a little one-sided."

"Joe is just…Joe. He was always better at taking than he was at giving." Mallory seized the opportunity to bring the subject around to what she'd wanted to discuss all along. She lowered her voice. "He's changed."

"In what way?" Dorian's interest seemed genuine.

"He's been different since the accident. Like a new man. A better man. The man he might have been if he hadn't made so many bad choices." Mallory detailed some of the major changes she'd observed over the past couple of weeks.

"So he has some kind of existential do-over thing going, huh?" Dorian asked.

Encouraged by Dorian's comment, she went on. "I've studied case histories of lightning-strike survivors. Many think they were allowed to live so they could right past wrongs."

Dorian's mouth twisted wryly. "If what I've heard about Joe is true, he has his work cut out for him. There's a lot of wrong to make right. I'll have to see it to believe it."

Mallory bit into a cookie. "You won't have long to wait. I'm due to meet him in town at noon. If Brindon finishes his business in time, maybe you two could join us for lunch and see what I'm talking about."

"Sounds good. I'm always hungry these days."

"You're eating for two," Mallory reminded.

"I know. I still can't believe it." Dorian rubbed her flat stomach tenderly. "It's not quite real to me yet."

"Then I guess you haven't experienced the joy of a little thing called morning sickness?" Mallory laughed.

"None at all. Is that bad?"

"No, that's good."

"You've piqued my curiosity about Joe." Dorian switched back to the subject they were discussing before she'd gotten distracted. "When Brindon told me he was staying here, I knew something had to be up. You're a very kind and giving person, Mal, but taking in the village loafer goes beyond generous. Are you bucking for Humanitarian of the Year?"

"He didn't have anyone else." Mallory recalled the nurse's

words back at the hospital. "A nice boy like that ought to have a lot of people worried about him." She felt a twinge of shame at her reaction. Judgmental and opinionated, she'd believed Joe incapable of change. His efforts to prove her wrong put her on the defensive. "He's not all bad. He's been…sweet. Almost courtly. He has very old-fashioned ideas about honor and respectability."

"Really?" Comprehension made her smile. "If you're not careful, I might think you're beginning to like the guy."

"I wouldn't say like," Mallory demurred. How could she? Like didn't begin to describe what she'd felt when they kissed. The lyrics of an old song tripped through her thoughts. Bewitched, bothered and bewildered. Yeah, that about summed it up.

"What *would* you say?" Dorian studied Mallory.

If she wasn't honest, her friend couldn't help her make sense of recent events, so she spoke before she could change her mind. "I've been experiencing some odd feelings lately. Odd for me anyway."

Dorian's carefully arched brows lifted. "Odd in what way?"

Mallory hesitated. This was how women bonded. By sharing their deepest feelings. Men had it easy. All they had to do was share a beer and, boom. Bonded. It was now or never.

A deep breath gave her the courage to plunge in. "For reasons I totally do not understand, I am insanely attracted to Joe Mitchum!" There. She'd said it. Out loud in broad daylight. No more pretending or denying her feelings.

To Dorian's credit, she didn't laugh or look too shocked by the startling revelation. Her eyes widened enough to reflect normal curiosity. "As in, physically attracted?"

"Yes, but it's more than that."

"Don't tell me you're attracted to his mind?"

"Actually, I am. It's weird. When he's near, and especially when I touch him, I get the eerie feeling that I couldn't *not* be attracted to him. Do you have any idea what I'm talking about?" The blonde nodded sympathetically, but the confu-

sion marring her model-perfect features told Mallory true understanding was not happening. "So say something."

"Uh, okay." Dorian grinned. "Love is blind? There's no
accounting for taste? Cupid has a twisted sense of humor?"

Mallory sent her friend a mock glare. "Contrary to what
you think, this is not funny."

Dorian smiled apologetically. "I'm still trying to process.
Honestly, I don't know what to say. The *very* last thing I
expected to hear coming out of Mallory Peterson's mouth is
the news that she has an itch for Joe Mitchum."

"You and me both."

"There must be more to tell," Dorian urged. "You can't
leave me hanging like this."

Oh boy, was there more. Mallory described the changes in
Joe's speech and mannerisms. How he had inexplicably gone
from uncouth to couth without passing go. Once she convinced
Dorian her observations were not the product of heatstroke or
low blood sugar, she explained the haunting scent of roses and
the déjà vu feelings she'd experienced.

"I'm totally freaked out," she concluded.

"Wow." Dorian exhaled on a slow breath. "I don't blame
you. But don't call the folks at *Unsolved Mysteries* just yet.
The problem may not as complicated as you think."

"Please explain it to me. I've lost enough sleep over this."

Dorian refilled their glasses. "I have more than one theory.
Which do you want first? Logical or illogical?"

"I'll take logical for $200, Alex."

Dorian grinned at the *Jeopardy* reference. "The logical explanation is that your biological clock is ticking. For all his
faults, Joe is a good-looking specimen with serious bad boy
charisma. You've spent a lot of time with him. You're feeling
a little, well…desperate. Basic biological math."

"That's your theory?"

"The keep-it-simple version."

"Let's try illogical for $400."

"This one's tougher. Maybe you feel a connection with Joe
because you saved his life. Living in such close proximity has

made you lose your objectivity and turn professional interest into something personal.''

"Makes sense, but it doesn't come near to explaining the roses. Go on.''

"Don't rush me. I only took one undergrad class in psychology, and it's been a while since I watched *Oprah*. How about if these weird manifestations are a result of your subconscious trying to rationalize your feelings. Since you obviously think Joe is wrong for you, your unconscious mind is sending you these pseudo messages of destiny so you won't feel too guilty when you actually fall into bed with the guy.''

Mallory hooted with laughter. "Right. Like *that's* gonna happen.''

"Don't rule him out completely,'' Dorian warned. "When I first met Brindon, I never imagined he would be my heart's mate. You have to look beyond the obvious.''

"Run your theory by me again. Is it my subconscious or my unconscious at work here? Because my conscious is really confused.''

"All right, make fun.'' Dorian flung up her hands. "That's the best I've got. If you're willing to drive to Dallas, I can give you the name of an excellent therapist.''

"So you think I'm crazy too? That's been my hypothesis all along.''

"I don't think you're crazy, Mallory.'' Dorian smiled. "Falling in love should be declared a mental illness, but as far as I know, it's still considered normal.''

"I am *not* falling in love with Joe Mitchum,'' she scoffed.

"Are you sure? Because that's what it sounds like.''

"I can't be.'' Could she?

"Why not?'' Dorian dusted cookie crumbs from the table.

Mallory's head tilted at a "puleese'' angle. "It's Joe. Do you have to ask?''

"You said he's changed.''

"He has. I think.''

"Or!'' Dorian's look was triumphant. "I've got it! Maybe it's *your* perception of *him* that's changed.''

Hmm. Mallory thought back over the past two weeks. How

many times had she contrasted the Joe who came home from the hospital with the Joe who'd climbed that utility pole? "No, it's not my imagination. He's definitely different."

Dorian sighed. "So why are you fighting your feelings?"

"Because people don't just change in the blink of an eye. Or in a flash of lightning."

"True," Dorian agreed. "It took me a lot longer. But then, I didn't have a million volts of electricity to light my enthusiasm. I thank my lucky stars every day that Brindon thought I could change. What if he'd given up on me?"

"He wouldn't have done that."

"Apparently, he never told you what a pain in the butt I used to be."

Mallory laughed at the other woman's honesty. She was all too familiar with the "opposites attract" scenario of the couple's courtship. She'd been shocked when Briny told her he was head over heels in love with the spoiled, self-centered ex-debutante petroleum princess. "So you believe people really can change?"

Dorian tapped her brow in a phony salute. "Lieutenant Living Proof reporting for duty."

Instead of answering her questions, Dorian's theory only created more. "So what should I do?"

"Be open to whatever develops. Give him a chance. Better yet, give yourself one."

Funny how it always came down to chances. Mallory couldn't decide which was more difficult—giving them, or taking them. "That's your advice?"

Dorian stepped around the table and gave her a warm hug. "Don't overthink this. Some things are better judged with your heart, not your head."

"Thanks." She couldn't decide if she was grateful or more perplexed.

"No problem." Dorian returned to her seat. "But hey, if that doesn't work out, I still have the therapist's number."

Mallory laughed again and tossed a wadded up paper napkin at her friend's head. Dorian's advice totally stunk, but she did feel better for having shared her feelings. "Call Brindon and see if he wants to meet us later."

Dorian retrieved a cell phone from her purse and punched the first number on auto dial. "Hi, sweetie. You still busy?" She smiled at Mallory and asked Briny if he was free for lunch. "I understand. Yes, I'll tell her. Hold on and I'll ask." She pressed the phone against her chest. "Is it all right if I hang out with you for a while?" When Mallory nodded, she spoke into the phone again. "That's fine. No, I'm sure Mallory won't mind. I know. I love you, too."

She ended the call and dropped the phone back into her chic little bag. "Brindon says hello, but it looks like we're on our own. After lunch, would you mind dropping me off at the bed and breakfast?"

"Of course not. But you two are welcome to stay here if you want."

"That's nice of you, but we've already booked a room. Newlyweds and all that. Oh, and you don't have to pick up Joe. He's with Brindon. You want to hear something really weird? They have 'business' to take care of."

"What kind of business?"

"He didn't say. Just that he needs to help Joe do something, and they'll be gone all afternoon. They're on their way to Lubbock."

"What in the world are they up to?"

Dorian reached for another cookie. "I don't know, and I didn't ask. It didn't take me long to learn the secret to a happy marriage."

"What's that?"

"Never get in my husband's way when he's determined to do a good deed."

It was early evening by the time Joe said goodbye to Briny, climbed into his truck and headed out to Mallory's. He still couldn't believe his good fortune. Thanks to Tucker, he was on the road to redemption. Hard to believe the old Joe could've made, much less kept such a friend, but he was glad to have a decent sort like Brindon Tucker in his camp.

Things were looking up, and for the first time since walking into his new life, he dared to believe he might yet make something out of the raw material he'd been given to work with.

When he arrived at Mallory's, he drove around back and parked. She was sitting in a canvas chair on the deck. She had a medical journal in her lap and one of the dogs at her feet. He climbed out of the truck. She stood and watched him walk up the graveled path, the setting sun burnishing her ginger-colored hair into a bright, burning halo. Light shone through her gauzy cotton dress, clearly outlining the shapely form beneath. He gazed at her for a long moment, bushwhacked by a hard rush of desire.

He no longer thought of her as she'd been before. He couldn't remember her other face or even recall the name she'd used. That life, those times, seemed so long ago and far away. This was the woman he wanted. The woman he needed to make his new life complete and obliterate all traces of the past.

Mallory was the one, the only one.

He smiled at her obvious consternation. She couldn't have looked more flabbergasted if he'd arrived wearing a whalebone corset and kid gloves. Once the initial shock passed, her golden brown eyes widened, turned warm and went soft by turns, as her appreciative gaze raked up and down the length of him. Desire stirred again, but this time it was stronger and deeper and harder to ignore.

Amazing what new clothes and the right woman's attention could do for a man's self-esteem. "Howdy, Ma'am."

"You've been shopping." Her voice was a whisper in the still twilight.

"It was about time." He reached down to pet the little white dog, which had turned out to be the most sociable member of the pack. It responded by thumping its tail against the deck. Two out of two were glad to see him.

"You've never dressed this way before." She might have meant to make an accusation, but the wonder in her words kept them from sounding critical.

He smiled. "You mean in clothes that aren't held together by sweat and wrinkles?"

"In western wear. I like the hat. Nice boots, too."

"Thank you. They seemed a good fit this morning, but I think they tightened up a mite as the day wore on." He stepped closer to breathe in the sweet scent of her, and she backed up.

Her head tipped toward the truck. "Where did you get that?"

"At the garage. Traded Bob the Jeep for it."

"I see. You've been busy today."

"There's still something I want to do." He reached out, lifted a soft curl from her cheek and tucked it behind her ear.

She shivered and twisted away from his touch like a calf from a branding iron. "Dorian said you and Briny went to Lubbock."

"We just got back."

"Oh?" She clutched the magazine to her chest like a shield while she perfected disinterest.

"Don't you want to know what we were doing?" he asked.

She shrugged. "It's probably none of my business."

"But it is. Everything I do is your business. You're part of who I am."

Her brows pulled down in confusion, and she shook her head as though refusing to accept the unbidden thoughts that filled it. "I'm sorry. What were you saying?"

"I appreciate all the hospitality you've shown me, but Briny insisted on helping me find a place of my own."

She'd turned to pluck a brown leaf from a geranium plant, but spun around at his words. "You're moving to Lubbock?"

If he didn't know better, he might think that was alarm in her voice. Would she mind if he left? He'd been so sure she'd be glad to see him go, considering how uncomfortable she'd been sharing her home with him these past weeks. "No. I'm not going anywhere. I still have a lot to do here."

"Oh." Funny how many different emotions could be expressed in a single syllable. That last one had been soaked in relief. "Like what?"

"There's so much you don't know." He had to be careful. Celestian had warned that revealing his true identity would be reason for recall. He could lose everything he'd fought for.

"Then tell me."

He longed to speak the words that were half-formed in his heart. But it was too soon, and if he didn't climb back on neutral ground, he might say something that would bring his house of cards tumbling down. "I'll be moving out on Monday."

She met his gaze and held it, the warm depths of her eyes revealing the exact moment when uncertainty was replaced by panic. She swallowed hard. "I don't understand."

"I know. I'm not used to how things are done either." He reached out to reassure her, to show her with a touch what he could not put into words. She trembled as a tingling arc of heat radiated from the spot where his skin connected with hers.

She pulled away. "What's going on, Joe?"

More than he could ever tell her. Knowledge might be power, but it was also a curse. People didn't know how lucky they were to be born ignorant of the past. "If I can trouble you for something cold to drink, I'll try to fill you in."

Chapter Eight

Mallory led the way inside. She'd spent the past two hours trying to study the latest developments in the treatment of otitis media in children under three, but was unable to concentrate. All she could think about was Joe and the "business" that had taken him to Lubbock. Why did she let herself get distracted by the man? She shouldn't be so interested in his activities.

She poured him a glass of lemonade, but when she set it down the drink splashed over the top. Frustrated, she grabbed a paper towel and swiped at the mess she'd made.

Joe hooked his new hat on the back of a kitchen chair and washed up at the sink. Taking a sip from his glass, he "much obliged" her. When he moved to stop her furious scrubbing with his free hand, self-preservation kicked in, and she dodged the contact.

"What is it?" he asked with a worried frown.

"Nothing." Too shrill.

"Have I done something wrong?"

She lowered her voice, switching to the calm tone she adopted when delivering bad news to patients. "You haven't done anything wrong. In fact, you seem to be doing everything right these days."

"And *that's* wrong?"

"Of course not. Well, yes. Maybe. Oh, I don't know!" So much for calm. The state was highly overrated anyway.

"What's got you so riled up?"

She stopped wiping the counter and tossed the sodden towel into the trash. "Riled up? Much obliged? Howdy, ma'am? You know, Marshal Dillon called. He wants his vocabulary back."

"Who?" He took another gulp of his lemonade, and she watched his Adam's apple bob. Fascinating. She'd never noticed how sexy a thyroid cartilage could be.

"Never mind." She was losing it. Totally. That's what happened when Joe got too close. Reason flew out the window. Insanity prevailed. The brain malfunctioned, and the hormones went native. Well, not this time. Chemistry would not triumph over common sense if she had anything to say about it. She stalked into the living room.

He followed her. "Let's sit down and cool off." His words were soft, soothing. "There's no problem so big it can't be talked out."

Oh, yeah? That's what he thought. Talking would not begin to solve her current problem. Only one thing would ease the tension building inside her. Tension that had maxed out in a hot flame of lust when he arrived dressed in crisp Wranglers and new boots. He looked like president-elect of the Cowboy Hunks of Texas Club. When had he become so damnably appealing?

His crooked, sexy smile made her mouth go dry. She should've poured herself a drink. A stiff shot of courage. If she had a sphygmomanometer handy, it would no doubt confirm a stress-related elevation in blood pressure accompanied by a racing pulse. A physical reaction that reinforced the startling discovery she'd made when she returned home after dropping Dorian at the bed and breakfast.

She hadn't been in the house ten minutes when she realized how quiet the place was without Joe's off-key whistling. How empty it felt without his big warm body around to take up space. As much as she hated to admit it, she had missed him today. She couldn't wait for him to get home.

Only this wasn't his home any longer. He was moving. Which was what she'd wanted all along. For two weeks, she'd prayed he would vacate the premises and park his disturbing presence elsewhere. So why did she feel so miserable at the thought he'd soon be gone?

Joe urged her to sit on the sofa, so she did. When he tried to settle beside her, she scooted to the other end and barricaded the space between them with pillows. Maybe by keeping a little distance between them, she could hang on to her good judgment. Judgment that eroded with every fluttery heartbeat.

The natives were definitely restless tonight.

Clearing her throat, she rubbed her damp palms on her skirt. "So you're moving out? Where to?" She feigned casual interest, grappling with self-control the way cowboys at the rodeo wrestled steers into submission.

"Briny got me another trailer." He grinned. "I mean modular home."

"That was good of him." She noticed a tiny bead of lemonade on his upper lip, and her finger itched to touch it. Instead, she toyed with the fringe on one of the pillows to keep her hands occupied.

"I told him I couldn't go along with the plan he cooked up unless I paid rent," Joe said. "I've already settled the first two months."

"Really?" As far as she knew, Joe had never given Briny a penny before for the privilege of squatting on the lot next door.

"Once I find a job and get some money ahead, I plan to make payments on the property." He leaned back, slid his arm along the back of the couch.

"You're buying the place?"

"It's high time I settled down. Briny's willing to carry the mortgage." He smiled half-heartedly. "I don't have a good credit standing in the community."

"Right." His determination to be a tax-paying property

owner was a shock. A bigger commitment than he'd ever been willing to make before.

"All that's fixing to change."

"So you're getting a new place?" And it wouldn't be so far away. Confused by the relief she felt, Mallory noticed a tiny scar like a pale apostrophe in the five o'clock shadow on Joe's chin. Why hadn't she noticed it before?

"The salesman called it a 'gently owned two-bedroom honey of a modular home.' He was keen for the cash transaction commission and promised to have it delivered, set up and tied down by close of business on Monday."

"Wow. How did Briny manage that?"

He smiled, and she knew what had caused the fine lines around his eyes. "He says money talks. I reckon it does, but most of the wheeling and dealing went over my head. I've never been on speaking terms with that kind of money, so I don't understand its language."

Mallory's laughter chipped away at her misgivings. Joe had always been quick with a quip, but even his humor was different now. The hard-edged sarcasm was gone, replaced by a gentler, almost homespun wit. "I'm glad you'll have a place of your own." That much was true. She *was* glad. As empty as the house would be, and as alone as she would be, once he was gone, her life could get back to normal.

So why did she always aspire to normalcy? What was so darned good about it? Normal was lonely. Empty. Normal meant focusing on healing others so she could deceive herself into thinking she was healthy. Normal. Not at all what it was cracked up to be.

"I put a few irons in the fire today." He grinned. "I meant what I said about taking care of the grounds. I'll start tomorrow. I got a line on some framing work today."

"That's great." And amazing. Joe had never shown much ambition.

"And all those broken automobiles over there?" His eyes warmed as he relayed his plans. "I talked to Bob down at the garage. He's gonna help me sell the parts. I'll clean up the lot, maybe plant some bushes. I have a plan, but I'm not ready to talk about it yet. I don't want to jinx it.''

Lost in her own thoughts, Mallory looked up as Joe's words took shape in her mind. He had a plan. Her heart turned over at the earnest, honest look on his face. Could it be true? Was he really trying to change? Maybe Dorian was right. Maybe all it took was the right set of circumstances to force a person to make a decision and stick with it. Much stranger things had happened.

So why was she so afraid to believe in him?

"Mallory?"

"Yes?"

"I want to thank you for everything you've done for me." He moved the pillows and slid down the sofa toward her. "If not for you I wouldn't be here."

"Just doing my job." She shifted uncomfortably. He was too close. She could smell the soap he'd used to wash his hands, but at least it wasn't rose-scented.

"I wasn't talking about you *making* me live."

"Then what?"

"If not for you, I wouldn't have a *reason* to live."

"Joe—"

"Shush." He placed his fingers on her lips to stop the words and moved closer. "I know I've made mistakes. More than a man's entitled to make in a lifetime. I won't ask you to over-look the past. What's done is done, and I can't change it. But is there any way you could bring yourself to think about the future instead?"

Mallory gulped to loosen the knot in her larynx. Thinking about the future might prove a little difficult since she was having so much trouble extracting herself from the moment. His gentle touch had ignited a riot of emotions inside her. Longing, desire, joy and sadness, exploding in turn like a string of firecrackers. She drew a deep breath, and the familiar scent of roses drifted out of nowhere.

Oh, boy, here we go again!

Her resistance evaporated, and she leaned toward him, pulled by a need stronger than any she'd ever known. Unable to tear her gaze from his, she saw a flicker of recognition reflected there. If eyes truly were the windows of the soul, the view from where she sat was incredible. She shivered in anticipation, and Joe pulled her close. As she settled into his embrace, all the taunting misgivings and doubts vanished like bubbles pricked by a child's eager finger.

Being with Joe was right. Loving him was what she was meant to do.

This was the way it had to be.

Mallory sighed in resignation as Joe's lips found hers. She was only human. How could she be expected to fight a force as powerful as fate?

Joe heard Mallory's soft sigh of surrender and felt the resistance melt out of her. He held her close and deepened the kiss, searching for the warmth he'd been denied during his century-long wait. He stroked her back in a slow caress. He was startled and excited by the realization that she wore no camisole or other undergarment. A wispy layer of cotton was all that lay between his questing hands and the warm flesh of her breasts. He hardened with desire as he worked the tiny buttons at the front of her dress.

His tongue slipped inside her mouth at the same moment his hand slipped inside her bodice. He cupped the fragile weight of her breast in his palm, and she moaned and gripped the front of his new shirt. She yanked and the snaps released with the popping sound of a miniature bullet hail. Her warm hands pushed the fabric apart to caress his chest.

She settled back against the cushions, pulling him down with her to stretch full-length on the sofa. When he realized the couch was too short for his long legs, he rolled to the floor in one fluid motion, bringing her down on top of him without breaking the weld of their kiss. Her bare breasts pressed against his chest, and her legs wedged between his. The denims that had fit so well when he bought them this morning were suddenly too tight and confining.

He reached down and fumbled past the full skirt tangled around her legs to caress the soft, warm skin of her thigh.

Thought was no longer possible. Blood had pooled in one part of his body, and it wasn't his brain. He stroked up her leg until he encountered the lace of her underwear. He'd seen half-naked women in lingerie ads on television, but seeing and touching were definitely different. His fingers slipped under the fabric and eased over the roundness of her bottom.

She moaned again, and her response only increased his desire. He wanted to feel more of her body, all of it. He wanted to taste every inch of her skin, discover all her hidden places and lose himself inside her.

Find himself.

She broke the kiss and rose up on hands planted firmly on each side of his head. She arched back, and the movement brought her breasts within kissing range. He drew one pink nipple into his mouth. When she cried out with shuddering pleasure, he turned his attention to the other. She was close to breaking. So was he. Too close. He gripped her hips under the skirt and rolled her onto her back. He held himself over her, pulsing with need and torn with indecision.

She stroked his chest, then the tense muscles of his back. Her hands slipped down, and her fingers ducked beneath the waistband of his pants. Thankfully, they were too tight to allow access. He was packing a loaded pistol that would fire wild if she touched him there.

He reclaimed her lips, his tongue dipping into her mouth the way he longed to dip into her body. Being with her so intimately was exciting, but discovering she wanted him as much as he wanted her…that was more than he had dreamed of.

The room grew dark as they lay on the floor exploring each other's bodies with hands and lips and tongues. Mallory was open to him, willing. Her tender sighs of pleasure told him he could claim her as his own. Remove the final barriers of clothing and inhibitions and take what she offered. What he had waited for and wanted so long.

But then what? She might be swept away tonight, but part of her intense response was a reaction to the lifetimes they'd shared. To the love they'd already made. The pull of eternal

love was usually all that mattered, but this time it wouldn't
be enough. Mallory was too logical, too grounded in her scientific ways to base a relationship on sex, even if that sex was
very, very good.

Come tomorrow and the bright light of day, she would regret allowing herself to give in to temptation. She'd regret the
sweet kisses and slow touches. She'd use their lovemaking
against him, as an excuse to turn away and reason herself right
out of his life. He didn't want to lose her, not now that he'd
tasted the heaven he'd found in her arms. He would wait until
he'd won her over on his own merit and convinced her he was
the kind of man she could respect.

Because with Mallory Peterson, without respect there could
be no love.

He rolled to his side, tucking her into the circle of his arms.
He brushed her face with a dozen little kisses and tenderly
rebuttoned her bodice and smoothed the skirt over her legs.
There wasn't much he could do about his own arousal except
wait for the blood to stop pounding.

"Joe?" she whispered.

"Yes?"

"Are we stopping?"

"Yes."

"Do you have a good reason?"

"I do."

"Care to share it?"

"I can't."

"Try."

He couldn't tell her the truth. That she was his other half,
and he'd made a special trip back to earth to be with her. Even
if such a revelation weren't against the rules, he couldn't speak
what was in his heart. She'd never believe him. Instead, he
expressed the thought that had given him the courage to end
their lovemaking.

"I don't want your body without your heart."

She turned her face into his chest and was silent for a long
time. It was too dark to see her face, but when she spoke, tears
trembled in her voice. "Do you mean that?"

"I'm not going to take the easy path and say I love you."

"You're not?"

"No, ma'am. What I mean to do is show you."

And that's how Joe spent the next three weeks. Once the new modular home had been set up and connected to utilities, he thanked her for her hospitality and moved out of her house. Shaken by what had almost happened on her living room floor, Mallory plunged herself into work, concentrating on her patients' problems to avoid dealing with her own. She saw Joe as he came and went next door, but their respective schedules left them little time to talk.

As promised, he took over grounds maintenance at the clinic, mowing the grass and weeding the flower beds in the early evening after a long day of framing houses. He refused to take money for his services, insisting he was just trying to repay her for taking him in when he had nowhere to go. She pointed out that he'd more than settled that score and was entitled to compensation for his efforts. Since the clinic was operating in the black, she convinced the board of directors to provide him a weekly retainer, so they wouldn't have to depend on townspeople to do the chores.

He found homes for four of the dogs, whittling the demon horde down to one—a little white dog he called by the odd name of Celestian. On his days off, Joe puttered around his place, cleaning up junk. Soon the hulking auto bodies had been carted away, either for parts or scrap metal. He traded a working engine from a wreck for an old riding lawn mower with a brush cutter, which he used to keep the two-acre lot tidy. Locals began hiring him to cut weeds on their rural properties. Those contacts led to other odd jobs, and before long, he was in steady demand.

When the house-framing job was finished, the contractor wrote him a letter of recommendation, which Joe proudly showed her. Mr. Peeler told him he'd be first on the rehire list when additional work came along. His efforts were beginning to pay off.

In fact, Joe Mitchum's magical transformation from dead-

beat slacker to super handyman was the talk of the town. Mallory's patients regularly offered opinions on the matter, rang-
ing from the pedantic "that lightning bolt must have knocked
some sense into him" to the pious "he's finally accepted the
spirit of the Lord." Regardless of what brought about the incredible change, the consensus seemed to be that Joe was well
on his way to redeeming himself.

Mallory knew what he was trying to prove and found no
peace from her own troubled emotions. She wasn't ready to
admit she loved Joe, but she was finally willing to admit she
could love him. Even though she'd disliked him in the past,
it had been his lifestyle she objected to. Maybe she had
jumped to conclusions in her typical judgmental way. She'd
always demanded perfection from herself, but it wasn't fair to
expect perfection from everyone else.

The prospect that she had come to care for him in their
short time together was frightening. But not nearly as frightening as the possibility that his unlikely rehabilitation could
be temporary. What if she got involved with him, and he hurt
her as he'd hurt everyone else who'd ever cared about him?

Finally understanding what the term "waiting for the other
shoe to drop" really meant, Mallory worried Joe might revert
to his old habits at the first sign of adversity. Things were
going his way now, but if the tide suddenly turned, would he
be strong enough to stick to his convictions?

She reveled in each small success because every step he
took forward put his life of dissolution farther behind him.
Being happy for him didn't make the return to solitary living
any more enjoyable. Frozen entrées for one were not nearly
as appetizing as the home-cooked meals he'd prepared. Having
the house to herself and more free time wasn't much fun either. Although she'd always made her own way in the world,
Mallory had never known what loneliness was until Joe
Mitchum blundered into her life.

"Joe, I appreciate your interest, but there's no way you can
throw your hat in the ring." The clerk at the election board

was kind enough not to let her surprise show too much when he'd walked in and stated his business.

"Do I need a law enforcement background to run for county sheriff?" He'd spent plenty of time maintaining law and order. But if he told the lady his experience came from his job as a Texas Ranger before the turn of the century, she'd call the keepers at the looney bin.

"No, that's not required. But you need a high school diploma. I was in your class, and I seem to remember you quit before graduation."

"Right." Folks were big on education these days. Finishing sixth grade had been an accomplishment in his last life; in fact, he'd had more schooling than most folks. When he'd joined the Rangers, few of his fellow lawmen could read or write. All he'd needed then was a steady aim, a sharp eye, devotion to justice and the willingness to risk life and limb for low pay. Everything had changed except the low pay part.

"Did you get your GED?" the clerk asked hopefully. "If you have your equivalency diploma, you can file a Declaration of Candidacy. There's a July deadline, though."

He doubted the old Joe had earned his high school certificate since he hadn't been what might be called highly motivated. Still, he didn't want to burn any bridges if there was a chance. He put on his hat and tipped his head respectfully in her direction. "I'll have to get back to you on that, ma'am."

Being a peace officer was all he really knew how to do. It was ironic that the one area in which he could truly succeed might be closed to him. He went home and worked in the yard, but couldn't get his mind off his disappointment. When he'd heard folks would vote in a fall election to choose a replacement for retiring county sheriff Nate Egan, he'd thought his prayers had been answered.

He'd make a good sheriff. As a Ranger, folks had claimed he was the toughest man west of anyplace east. He wasn't brutal or hotheaded like some men, but once he found a scent, he didn't give up till he tracked down his prey. Persistence was a good trait for a sheriff. The steady job would enable him to save the money he needed to build a real house that he'd be proud to offer Mallory. He was making progress convincing her he'd changed, but wearing a sheriff's badge would put him over the top. A lawman, elected by a vote of the people, was a respected member of the community. And about as different from the old Joe as he could get.

He didn't doubt he could do the job. Keeping the peace in Slapdown nowadays wouldn't be nearly as dangerous as it had been then. For one thing, he wouldn't have to spend days in the saddle, trailing rustlers and gunmen. The sheriff drove a specially marked car with a siren and flashing lights.

He dusted the dirt from his hands and backed up to survey his work. The place was shaping up. He'd bought enough lumber to build a stoop on the front, using the deck behind Mallory's house as a template. After painting the shutters dark gray, he planted a row of boxwoods and pots of marigolds around the skirting and made a walk of crushed gravel that ran from the new parking area to the front steps. He'd mowed the area between the road and the house, and even though the new lawn was mostly weed, it looked neat and cared-for.

The additions made the place less temporary, and more like a real home. Not that he planned to live in it forever. He'd already picked out a spot for the house he'd build someday, but when he purchased the deck materials at the home center in Midland, he'd been shocked by the high cost of supplies. He'd have to save a considerable amount before he could break ground.

A dream gave a man something to work for.

Celestian the dog rose from his favorite spot by the front step and stretched. The little fella didn't seem to miss his noisy companions much and had turned out to be a loyal pooch. He'd had to find new homes for the rest of the animals. One dog might be man's best friend, but five were nothing but a nuisance.

It had been a little trickier to rid himself of Joe's former lady friends. Every time he went to town, some loose-looking woman approached him and invited him out. Or in. It had taken some doing to convince them he was no longer interested in keeping company with them. Glorieta Tadlock had been the toughest nut to crack. The gum-snapping chippie had taken the news hard and had even shed a tear or two when he'd told her he needed to break off whatever they'd had in the past.

He went inside for a drink of cold water and was still at the sink when he heard a knock on the door. Answering it, he found a dark-haired woman in a denim skirt and pink shirt on the step. Behind her, a little girl with bobbed-off blond hair knelt to pet the dog. "Can I help you?"

The woman glared at him. "Well if you did, it'd be the first time." She shoved the door and pushed past him into the house. "Nice place you got here."

"Thank you." He was used to being accosted by Joe's female friends, but this one was new to him. He'd never seen her before, but she didn't look like the others.

"What the hell's going on here?" A good six inches shorter than him, she gamely stood her ground and poked a finger into his chest.

"I don't know what you mean."

She looked at him long and hard, like she was measuring him for a coffin. "Are you all right?"

"I am now."

"No permanent damage from being struck by lightning?"

"No."

"Good. Because I'm gonna kill you."

"Now wait a minute." He could only imagine how the old Joe might have mistreated the poor woman. Apparently, he'd been particularly gifted at making female enemies.

"What is all this?"

"All what?"

She spun around, taking in the parlor which had come furnished with blue and tan furniture and looked passably nice, if he did say so himself. "This! What do you think you're doing living like this?"

"I got tired of camping out." He had to be careful. The little lady looked like the easily provoked type.

"How come you haven't called?"

"I don't have a phone." Since he had no idea who she was, he couldn't have called her if he'd had the means.

The woman sighed and her shoulders slumped, as though most of the fight had leaked out of her. She sounded tired when she spoke. "I don't expect anything from you, Joe. I gave up on that a long time ago. When we broke up, just getting out with my heart in one piece was good enough for me. But that doesn't mean you don't owe Chloe."

She walked to the storm door and looked out at the little girl who was trying to make Celestian chase her by running in circles.

As he watched, the child picked up a stick. She drew back her tiny arm and flung it less than a foot. The dog's head swung from the girl to the stick, but didn't make the connection. He sat on his rump and stared up at her expectantly, his pink tongue lolling.

Joe's breath caught when the child turned and waved at the woman. Chloe. He recalled the name the same moment he recognized the little girl's dark eyes and full lips. They were a miniature version of his own.

"Dammit, Joe." His ex-wife, Brandy by name, whacked him on the arm. "Chloe is your daughter. When are you going to start acting like her father?"

Chapter Nine

"Don't just stand there." The foot Brandy stamped let Joe know she'd run out of patience. "Talk to me."

He shifted his weight, looked down at his boots, and up at the woman who'd waltzed him into a corner. What could he say? He'd known about the little girl. Mallory had mentioned Joe's daughter, and he'd found a photograph of a plump infant in the box from the salvage yard. Like so many aspects of the life he'd been thrust into, fatherhood hadn't seemed real to him before. Not until this moment.

He wasn't surprised the old Joe had shirked his parental responsibilities. Still, his gut tightened with shame to think everyone, including the little girl, believed he'd turned his back on her. There was no excuse for neglecting a child, and he wouldn't insult her mother by making one. "I haven't done right by...Chloe. For that I am truly sorry."

Brandy started to speak, then stopped and did a double take. "What?"

"I've messed up worse than a hen in a dung heap." He expected the old familiar sayings to fade like the memories, but they still cropped up when he least expected them. "I haven't been a good father," he clarified.

"Finally! A fact we can agree on." She threw up her hands in mock amazement. "But I didn't expect you to give in so quickly. I came braced for a fight. Why aren't you arguing with me?"

"Hard to argue with the truth."

Her laugh was bitter. "Never stopped you from trying before."

"I hope it's not too late for me to make amends."

"You mean that?" Uncertainty tinged her words; doubt underlined them.

"Yes, ma'am." That's what his life was all about this time around. Making amends. For three weeks, he'd worked to repair the damage the old Joe had caused so he could win back his lost respect. In the end, earning the trust of a tiny girl and her suspicious mother was far more important than regaining the confidence of the folks in town.

"If it's not too late, I want things to be different with her." He tipped his head toward the door. Outside, the little girl had lost interest in the impromptu game of fetch. She crouched on her haunches in the freshly turned dirt of the flower bed, fascinated by a wriggling earthworm.

"Dammit, Joe, why do I want to believe you?" Tears welled up in Brandy's eyes. When they rolled down her cheek, she wiped them with the back of her hand and paced in a tight circle. "After all you've put me through, taking you at your word now means I gotta be crazy, right?"

"No," he said softly. "It means you're forgiving and trustful and generous. The kind of woman I want raising…our daughter."

Brandy stared at him for a long moment. When she spoke, her voice was choked with emotion. "You really have changed."

"I'm trying."

"You look different, sound different." She tilted her head and peered at him. "Are you taller?"

"I don't think so."

"I heard the accident turned you around, that you've been

working and living right. I didn't believe it, but now that I've seen you and this place…I'm more confused than ever."

"You're doing okay." He patted her arm. What he said wasn't as crucial as how he said it. A soft voice and softer touch could reassure the most skittish mare. This wasn't the first time he'd used his old skills. Just last week he'd been cutting brush around the training ring at a rural horse farm when he'd stepped in to help the handler calm a worked-up filly.

"It's just hard to get past the lying and cheating and hurting, you know? I can't even count all the times you disappointed Chloe."

"I wouldn't blame you if you couldn't find it in your heart to forgive me," he told her softly. "But I hope you can."

She drew a deep shuddering breath. "God help me, I think you mean it. Actions speak louder than words, right?"

"That's what I'm counting on." He sensed her defenses dropping. She warmed to him and came around to a new way of thinking, just as others in town had done. Not everyone fought the feelings as hard as Mallory.

"Deep down, something tells me you're being sincere. You sincere? Who'd have thought?" She pressed a hand over her mouth and stared at him as though searching for the truth in his eyes. In his heart.

"Thank you for believing in me. I promise I won't let Chloe down this time." He met Brandy's gaze with a calm he didn't feel. He had a hatload of secrets about his true identity. Secrets that would isolate him in the world. Still, he meant what he said. Chloe deserved a better father than Joe had been. If a little girl couldn't depend on her daddy, who could she depend on?

Brandy released a pent-up breath. "That makes me feel a lot better about what I came here for."

"What's that?" He hoped she didn't want to pick up the pieces of their shattered marriage. Unlike most of the females in Joe's life, Brandy seemed like a nice woman, and he didn't want to hurt her. Again. Neither did he want to rekindle the past.

"I need you to keep Chloe for me. I've never pressed you about extended summer visitation, even though it's provided for in the divorce decree. You haven't had a decent place for her stay before, but this one's nice. Mind if I look around?" Without waiting for permission, Brandy began her inspection, opening closets, looking behind closed doors and checking the contents of cupboards. "You even have an extra bedroom. Yes, this'll do just fine."

Joe panicked. He was all for establishing a bond with the little girl who thought he was her father. But taking care of her? His body had supplied half the raw material that made her, but he didn't know a blasted thing about children, especially tiny females. "I'm sorry I can't keep her. I have to work."

Brandy's eyes narrowed. "No, you don't. I checked. That framing job is finished. That's why I'm here. I've never asked you for anything, but I'm asking now. I've been accepted to paralegal school, but I need time to study and attend classes. I want a real job that pays more than minimum wage. You don't begrudge me that, do you?"

"Well, no. But what about her grandparents?" He recalled Mallory saying the two had been living with Brandy's mom and dad for several months.

"Mom had back surgery. Dad's got his hands full taking care of her. They do more than their share. It's your turn. All I'm asking for is a month."

"What?" She expected him to tend the child for a whole month? Didn't she know he wasn't qualified? Being the oldest of a passel of brothers and sisters back on the farm hardly made him an expert. Those days were long gone, and memories of them grew paler each day.

"You haven't had her overnight once in two and half years. A month won't kill you, and it'll give me time to settle into my new schedule. I'm trying to build a life for our daughter…the kind of life she deserves." Brandy opened the refrigerator, peered inside, and then glanced up with an incredulous look. "You cook now?"

"Some."

"Will wonders never cease?" She pulled a sheaf of papers out of her purse. "I've written down everything you need to know. What Chloe likes to eat, what she won't touch, etc. I've outlined her bed and bath routines and listed her favorite stories and games, but feel free to start your own traditions. Kids are flexible and always interested in new things."

"Wait, Brandy. Can we talk about this?"

"No, Joe, we can't." She slung her purse strap over her shoulder. "Talk was always what you did best, but it won't cut it this time. You're going to have to *do* for a change and take some responsibility." She thrust the papers at him.

A long finger of dread clawed across his belly as he took the folded sheets. "When do you want her to come?"

Brandy laughed. "Honey, she's here. Her stuff's in the car." She stepped out on the stoop. "Chloe, baby, Daddy says he's tickled pink to have you stay with him so Mommy can start school."

Chloe pushed herself off the ground with her hands and dusted them on the seat of her short red pants. She stared at Joe, her dark eyes narrowing. "Do I hafta stay wif him?"

"Just for a little while, sweetie. Remember, we talked about how much Daddy misses you." Brandy gave Joe an apologetic look. "She'll be fine once I'm out of sight. It's hard for her to separate. Use Dr. Peterson's phone to call if you have a problem. My class schedule is on the paper."

The child ducked behind her mother's skirt. "He's not Daddy."

Brandy laughed. "Wow, Joe. You've changed so much your own flesh and blood doesn't recognize you." She pulled her skirt from the little fist and placed Chloe's hand in Joe's. "You two get reacquainted while I bring in her things." She headed for the car.

Joe's breath caught in his throat. He had a child. A walking, talking human being with wants and needs he couldn't begin to comprehend. A tiny stranger who depended on him for everything. Without the luxury of familiarity, he was bound to make mistakes. Being a good father was the most important job a man could ever have, and yet he had no training, no skills and no experience. Chloe's hand felt fragile in his, her bones as thin and fine as a bird's. He suspected her heart would be as easily broken.

He didn't know what to say, so he stated the obvious. "So, you're Chloe."

She nodded and looked up at him with wide brown eyes set in a heart-shaped face. She sported a turned-up nose, round pink cheeks and sun-streaked blond hair cut bluntly above her brows and bowled-off just below her ears. "Yep. Who're you?"

Her question startled him, and for a moment, he didn't know how to respond. "I'm...Daddy."

She shook her head, her expression solemn. "Nuh-uh."

He swallowed hard. Was it possible? Could this innocent child somehow sense the switch that had brought him here? Had he successfully fooled everyone into thinking he was the new and improved Joe Mitchum, only to be unmasked by a stubborn three-year-old skeptic? Maybe she didn't have the mind-set to rule out the impossible. Maybe she trusted her intuition, as adults seemed unable to do.

"Are you a nice man?" Chloe nailed him with directness.

Brandy walked up, her arms full of bags and blankets and toys. She laughed nervously. "Of course Daddy's a nice man, honey. He loves you just as much as Mommy does. He's been really, really busy getting his house fixed up so you could come and visit. I know he's going to take good care of you, and you two are going to have a wonderful time together."

"Okay." Chloe continued to stare up at him. He hoped Brandy left before the child said anything else to arouse her mother's suspicions. He might be forbidden to tell the truth, but lying to a three-year-old didn't feel right either.

Brandy shifted the burden in her arms and looked over her daughter's head. "I'm trusting you with the one person who's most precious to me."

"I understand."

"Good, I hope so. There's a lot riding on this. For all of us." Brandy hugged and kissed her daughter, said goodbye and climbed into the car. She gave final instructions through the rolled-down window. "You may not get another chance with her, Joe, so whatever you do, don't blow it."

Always the last to leave the clinic, Mallory took the final phone call of the day. When she hung up, she leaned back in her chair with her hands behind her head. Brandy Mitchum had left little Chloe with Joe and phoned to ask if Mallory would check in regularly to make sure he took good care of the girl. She'd given the uneasy mother her word, so she locked up and headed next door.

The silly little dog greeted her with a friendly sniff and danced around her legs until she reached down and scratched his head. Satisfied, he dashed ahead and plopped down in front of the door. Alerted by the barking, Joe stepped out on the porch.

"Hey, there, Mallory." There was no mistaking his wide grin. He was happy to see her.

"Hello, Joe." How was it possible for him to look even better than she remembered? Working in the sun had bronzed his skin and toughened the muscles under the black cotton T-shirt stretched across his chest. Judging from the stylish cut, a professional had trimmed his dark hair recently, revealing threads of premature silver that shone in the sunlight.

"You've been keeping yourself pretty scarce lately, Doc."

"Busy, you know."

"Come on in." He stepped back and held the door.

The first thing she noticed was the mouthwatering aroma of roasting chicken. It wafted out of the small kitchen into the living room where Chloe was sprawled on the carpet, playing with plastic farm animals. Sections of miniature fencing surrounded a red toy barn. Tiny ducks and geese swam in a blue plastic pond.

The little girl looked up and grinned. "Hi, Docker P."

"Looks like you're having fun." She knelt on the floor beside Chloe.

"Joe helped me make a farm. See, here's the piggies and the chickies."

She looked up at him, her brows quirked in question. "Joe?"

He winced. "She doesn't want to call me daddy."

"Ah. Well, maybe in time." She stood. "Who'll watch her if you get another job?"

"I guess I won't be working for the next month. Except around here."

"If you need a short-term baby-sitter, my office manager's daughter could probably help you out. She's fifteen and reliable."

"Thanks. I'll keep her in mind."

Chloe yanked on Mallory's trouser leg. "Wanna see my new room?"

"Sure." The child took her hand and pulled her into the extra bedroom Joe had prepared for her. He'd hung her clothes neatly in the closet and stacked her picture books on the bedside table.

"This is nice. You have a lot of toys."

"Uh-huh. I brung 'em wif me 'cause Joe didn't have any."

Mallory smiled. It certainly didn't take long for a little girl to stake out her territory. Dolls and teddy bears and blocks lay scattered around the mint-green room. "Looks like you and your daddy have been having fun."

Chloe shrugged, her thin shoulders rising almost to her ears. "Joe's nice. But he's not my daddy."

"Of course, he is. He just looks different."

"Nope." Chloe shook her head stubbornly. "But I like him anyways."

Mallory knelt until they were eye to eye. "Your daddy's trying to make up for all the times he couldn't be with you." At least that's what her mother had told Mallory on the phone. Considering Joe's track record, Brandy hadn't seemed too worried about letting him care for the child. "You're his little girl, and he wants you to be happy."

"I know, but he's not my daddy. You wanna eat wif us? Joe's cookin' chicken. He let me rub stuff on it."

"Oil and pepper," he said from the doorway. "We have plenty, if you'd like to stay for supper."

"Thanks, but I can't." She'd managed to avoid him since the night they'd almost crossed the line on her living room floor. She'd been all too willing to give herself to him then, but her impetuous behavior had seemed incredibly wrong the next day. Joe had been a womanizer, both before and after his divorce. He claimed to be trying to break old habits, but if she succumbed to his charm, the only thing that would get broken was her heart.

Considering they were neighbors in a very small town, total evasion had been impossible, but by rationing her time between the clinic and home, she'd done a fair job of staying out of his way. Until now.

"Can't stay?" he asked with a crooked grin. "Or are you afraid to?"

Terrified. She'd missed him the last few weeks. More than she thought possible. More than she cared to admit. "Shouldn't."

"Chloe doesn't bite, do you, tadpole?"

"Nope." The little girl giggled. "Stay, Docker P. and eat chicken wif us."

"Well—"

"Pleeease."

How could she say no when resistance spelled another solitary evening? "All right. I'd be honored to have dinner with you, Chloe."

The little girl bounced up and down. "Goody!"

"And this way you'll be able to give her mother a full report." Joe winked knowingly.

"What?" Her nerve endings tingled in response to his lazy smile. Maybe staying wasn't such a good idea after all.

"I figure you're here for a reason." His husky drawl was honey-coated. "Isn't that reason's name Brandy?"

She nodded. "Busted. She was a little nervous about leaving Chloe."

"Can't say I blame her. Don't know how the next thirty days will go, but for the moment, we're good. Right, tadpole?"

The silly nickname made Chloe giggle. "Right, Joe!"

After a tasty meal of seasoned chicken roasted with new potatoes and carrots, Mallory allowed herself to be persuaded to stay a little longer. Now that she'd experienced the pleasure of Joe and Chloe's company, she was even more reluctant to leave the warmth and laughter and return to a house that had been unbearably empty since Joe moved out. For now, it was enough to sit in the background and watch him interact with his daughter.

Once again, he was a total surprise. According to Brandy, prior to the accident Joe hadn't known how to relate to his daughter, nor had he shown much interest in spending time with her. That assessment didn't jibe with what she'd observed tonight. She could report back to Brandy that although Joe acted a little awkward and unaccustomed to dealing with the child, his tender concern and affection were genuine.

Mallory sat at the foot of the bed while he read Chloe a bedtime story about a little rabbit that wanted red wings. When he reached the end, he closed the book, pulled the sheet up to her chin and stood to leave.

"You're 'posed to kiss me good-night," Chloe reminded patiently.

"Oh, right. Sorry." He bent low and pecked her forehead. "Good night."

Chloe extended her hand, palm up. "Don't forget."

"What?" He looked at Mallory and she shrugged.

"Gimme your hand," Chloe commanded. She held his large hand in both her tiny ones, bent her head over it and pressed a damp kiss in the middle of his palm. Then she curled his fingers over it. "There. You're 'posed to save that one for later. Mommy says one kiss isn't enough to last through the night."

"Oh. Right. Thanks." He held his hand against his chest. When Chloe continued to look up at him, he sighed. "What?"

"Aren't you gonna gimme one for later?"

He turned to Mallory, and she encouraged him with a look. "Sure. I was just about to do that." He complied, and Chloe's small fist closed tightly. He gave her a teddy bear to hug and re-tucked the sheet.

"Ni-night, Joe. Ni-night, Docker P."

"Good night." Mallory's chest ached with the proof of Joe's tenderness. He might not have been there for Chloe in the past, but the scene she'd just witnessed made her think he wanted to make up for lost time.

"Sleep tight, Chloe," Joe whispered as he turned out the light.

Mallory insisted on washing the dishes while he enjoyed another cup of coffee. When she asked how he'd equipped the kitchen, he extolled the virtues of the local thrift store where he'd found most of the dishes and pans. Dot at the diner had tipped him to the bargains and had contributed a few second-hand items like sheets and towels. As Mallory dried the dishes and put them away, she marveled at how well he managed with the bare necessities.

"It's odd that Chloe calls you Joe instead of Daddy."

"Daddy's a title I have to earn." He stretched out his long legs and ran a hand through his hair. "If anyone can make me earn it, that little girl can."

"Are you sure you're up to a month of playing the role?"

"I don't know. I'll just have to take things one day at a time."

"Let me know if there's anything I can do to help." She dunked the roasting pan into the soapy water.

"Well, as a matter of fact, there is something I've been meaning to ask." He took a sip of the coffee she'd poured. "What in tarnation is a GED?"

She scrubbed the pan. "I think it stands for general equivalency diploma. It's what people earn in lieu of a high school diploma."

His eyes widened with what could only be described as hope. "You mean even if I didn't finish high school, I can get the paper?"

"Sure. People do it all the time." Strange that he wouldn't know that. She dried the pan and put it away.

"How does it work?"

Mallory sat down at the table and told him what she knew

about the GED program. When she asked what had prompted his interest, he told her about his visit to the election board.

With Joe, it was just one surprise after another. Sheriff. Joe? She had never guessed he harbored such ambition. "Are you serious?"

"You don't have to sound like doubting Thomas." His mock indignation told her he wasn't really offended. "I may have made a profession out of shiftlessness, but I never broke any laws. Did I?"

"No," she agreed. "If we don't count 'borrowing' electricity."

His lopsided grin made her heart beat faster. "That's history."

"What makes you think you can do the job?"

"I respect the law and want to serve it." He paused. "I have a selfish motive, too. I'd like to be part of the community. I'm tired of living on the edge, never belonging anywhere."

"That's admirable, Joe, but aren't you afraid of…biting off more than you can chew?"

"You don't think I have a snowflake's chance in the Mojave of winning that election, do you?" He swirled the contents of his coffee cup.

"I didn't say that." But she had thought it.

"You think I'm reaching too far." The guarded, wounded look was back. "Wanting too much."

His words sounded oddly familiar. She'd said that very thing, once upon a time. As a poor girl from a working-class home, she had reached for the stars when she decided to become a doctor. It was her good fortune that the people who mattered most had believed in reaching, too. They hadn't dashed her hopes. She couldn't dash Joe's. "There's no such thing as wanting too much. My parents always told me, if you can dream it, you can make it happen."

He repeated the sentiment, almost to himself. "Problem is, I can dream it, but I can't make it happen without you."

She would help him because she never could have realized her own dreams without the willing help of others. "Just tell me what I can do."

"For starters, explain how I can get that GED thing."

"Hmm. It'll require a lot of study and hard work. It's been a long time since you were in school."

He rolled his eyes wryly. "You have no idea how long. Since I can't take a regular job while I have Chloe, now would be a good time for me to stay home and study, right?"

"I suppose so." It was odd that he'd never looked into this before.

"The deadline for filing a Declaration of Candidacy is in July," he told her.

"Wow, that doesn't give you much time, but since you've already earned most of your high school credits, it may be long enough. You'll need to go to the high school right away and talk to the director of the GED program, find out which courses you need to complete."

"I can do that." He jumped up. "Wait, let me get a pencil and paper. I don't want to forget anything."

She smiled when he returned. "You're really serious about this, aren't you?"

"Dead serious."

She studied him as he made careful notes about his election plans. His face was honest and open. Gone was the who-cares attitude and in-your-face smirkiness that had grated on her nerves in the past. What had happened to the old Joe Mitchum? Who was this amiable, hardworking stranger? Could Chloe be right? Was it possible that Joe simply wasn't Joe?

She had to admit he was more than a new man. He was a different man. A better man than he'd ever aspired to be. So what had happened? Could a lightning bolt really effect such a change? Or had a look-alike taken his place sometime between falling off the utility pole and hitting the ground? As crazy as it sounded, that would explain not only the reversal of personality, but also his fish-out-of-water behavior. A pod-person theory would account for his newly developed conscience, unexpected ambition and the bizarre claim made by one of her rancher patients that Joe Mitchum was the "best darned horse gentler" he'd ever come across.

A horse gentler? Since when?

Most important of all, the replacement-Joe theory made sense of the powerful emotions he evoked in her. It might even explain her need to kiss him, when she knew how dangerous it would be to go there again. Dorian had warned her about justifying her feelings. Was that what she was doing with all this wild conjecture?

Talk about reaching. If Joe wasn't Joe, who the heck was he? And why would anyone want to step into his meaningless life?

She gave herself a mental shake. There was nothing weird going on. The simple explanation was the best. A life-affirming accident had opened Joe's eyes. There was nothing mysterious about hard work and fence-mending. He'd already come a long way in making himself over. It was clear he thought being elected sheriff would be the ultimate accomplishment.

The only strange thing at work here was the fact that a bolt of lightning had set them both on such unexpected paths. If anyone had told her a month ago she'd be sitting at Joe Mitchum's kitchen table helping him plot an election campaign strategy, she would have prescribed antipsychotic medication.

Then again, she'd always been a sucker for a challenge.

Joe finished writing and looked up. "After I get the GED, what do you think my next move should be?"

"Tell you what. You get signed up for the program, and I'll help you study. I think most of the classes are held at night at the high school. I'll even come over and stay with Chloe while you attend."

"You'd do that for me?" His gratitude was almost her undoing.

"What are neighbors for?" she asked with a grin.

"You don't think I'm barking up the wrong tree?" He reached across the table and placed his hand on hers, as though needing reassurance only she could give him. "Am I a fool to want what might be beyond my reach?"

She couldn't deny the unmistakable warmth emanating from his touch. She breathed deeply, waiting for the roses. She'd been foolish herself once. She'd burned to be a doctor when a wiser person would have considered her goal impossible. But others had shared her dream, and because of that she had made it come true. Joe had already demonstrated he wasn't afraid of hard work. Maybe all he needed was someone to share his dream.

"No, Joe." Unable to resist the magnetic pull, she reached up and stroked her hand along his jaw. "You're not a fool. And I think you're barking up the *right* tree."

Chapter Ten

First thing the next morning Joe stopped by the administration office of the Slapdown Independent School District and registered for the GED program before he could back out and change his mind. He was worried about putting his century-old knowledge up against the current high school curriculum. Revealing the extent of what he didn't know might raise suspicions, but he had to try. What good would another chance do him, if he wasn't man enough to take it?

With Chloe in tow, he filled out the paperwork and waited nervously while program director Alice Stringer checked the records at Slapdown High.

What she discovered was encouraging. Joe had withdrawn from school only a few weeks short of graduation, but that wasn't the best news. Before dropping out, he had somehow managed to complete all of the school district's required courses except the second semester of twelfth grade English.

Maybe the dream wasn't beyond his reach after all.

Because he was facing a tight deadline, Mrs. Stringer placed him in an accelerated program, which required him to attend evening classes three nights a week for three weeks. If he made passing grades on the English assignments, earned at least a C on the required research paper and passed the general education review, he would receive his diploma in time to file a Declaration of Candidacy with the election board.

Joe had received his formal education in a one-room schoolhouse. He was a bit overwhelmed by the complexities of a modern school system but was determined to make good on the opportunity that had dropped into his lap. Winning Mallory's respect was the best shot he had at overcoming the biggest obstacle to their love—her lack of faith in him. Despite their powerful physical attraction, she was afraid to trust him and was unwilling to believe the changes he'd made were permanent.

If he earned his diploma, he could run for sheriff. If he ran, he would win because losing was not a consideration. As sheriff, he'd have a respectable job and a permanent place in the community. With a solid future to offer, he could court Mallory in earnest. If he won her heart, they could live out their days on earth and spend eternity together.

It sounded simple enough, but there were a lot of ifs. Too many. Only one thing in life was certain, and he'd already had a taste of death. The experience had taught him the importance of making the most of every moment. Whether his plan was a well-thought-out strategy or a crazy pie-in-the-sky scheme, it was his only hope.

With books and reading assignments in hand, Joe approached Mallory about staying with Chloe during his night classes. Openly impressed by the initiative he'd shown in getting into the program, she kept her promise to baby-sit and renewed her offer to help with his studies. If she was unable to get away from work on time, he could drop Chloe at the clinic, and she could play in the children's area of the waiting room until Mallory was free.

With no time to lose, Joe started classes right away. Most nights, he returned home long after Mallory had tucked Chloe into bed. Sometimes she stayed, and they ate popcorn and studied together at the kitchen table. It was hard to concentrate with her so close he could smell her rain-scented hair, and he had to struggle to keep his mind on the homework. It was darned hard to focus on American literature when all he could think about was how Mallory had sighed in surrender at his touch.

However, he'd promised to show her how much he loved her, and he always kept his word. Making decent grades was the first step in that direction, so he forced his mind back to his studies as Mallory quizzed him on the readings. As they went over historical facts, basic mathematics and scientific concepts for the high school review test, he discovered the most difficult part of attaining an education was not learning new things; it was concealing how little he really knew.

A lot had happened during the twentieth century, but he'd paid sporadic attention to the droning current events monitor in the time-out room. If he hadn't kept current with what was going on in the world, he never could have caught up on a hundred years in three weeks.

Evenings were consumed with classes and study. Days he tended Chloe and worked at sprucing up the yard and clearing away the last of the junk autos. As word got out, more and more handyman jobs came along, in town and on neighboring farms. When possible, he took Chloe with him and used their time together to memorize lessons by sharing them with her. Helping him made her feel important, and reciting facts aloud made it easier to commit them to memory. Though he was often exhausted from lack of sleep, he pulled out his books and read during Chloe's afternoon naps, forging ahead in an attempt to complete the program in time.

His dedication paid off in unexpected ways. He'd worried that when people found out what he was trying to do they would belittle his efforts. After all, the old Joe hadn't exactly been a staunch pillar of the community. He was well aware that his unlikely transformation from ne'er-do-well to upstanding citizen was a lot for the average person to digest.

He underestimated the good people of Slapdown. Everywhere he went, folks shook his hand and pounded him on the back and swore that if he managed to make it into the sheriff's election, he could have their votes. While he wanted to believe such heartfelt encouragement was a sign he was on the right track, given Joe's reputation, he didn't understand why the support was forthcoming.

Dot set him straight when he stopped by the diner one afternoon. "So you're really gonna run for sheriff, huh?" the waitress asked.

"That's the plan." He sipped a cup of coffee while Chloe perched on the stool beside his and slurped a strawberry milkshake.

"I hear you're knocking 'em dead in those night classes."

He grinned, as embarrassed by the compliment as he had been when Mrs. Stringer took him aside to commend his efforts. "I'm doing my best."

"Folks are rooting for you. You're a local man. Your people have lived in these parts for a long time. Four generations, right?"

"Thereabouts." He'd perfected several noncommittal responses that served him well when people asked for information he had no way of knowing.

"Your great-granddaddy helped get this town started," Dot went on. "The Mitchum name has always been as good as gold around here."

"Until I knocked the shine off it." He'd probably never know what had set Joe on the wrong path; that information had died with the man in whose mortal coil he now dwelled. Walking-in could buffalo a man. Celestian should work up a handbook to help the poor, unsuspecting souls who stepped into the lives of others. What he needed was a guide to bridge the gap and fill in the holes. As it was, he didn't know why Joe had taken a wrong turn after starting off so well.

Dot dabbed a speck of ice cream off Chloe's nose with a paper napkin. "We all make mistakes, Joe, some of us more than others. I'm just glad you're finally pulling yourself up. I know you took it hard when your daddy died. Your mama worried about you right up until she passed. But life is for the living."

Even if he had to live it in another man's body. "I'm grateful for the opportunities I've had." Every day he thanked his lucky stars for this additional time on earth. Time he could spend with Mallory. The bell over the door jingled, and he tensed, fearing Glorieta Tadlock might have followed him into the diner again. The last time they spoke, he'd tried to make it clear he wasn't interested in renewing their acquaintance, but her fawning response had told him she wasn't ready to give up.

When he turned and saw Bob and his mechanic enter, Joe let out a relieved sigh. They called to him, and he raised his hand in acknowledgement. "How're you boys doing?"

"Pretty good. You still hitting the books?" Bob's question was friendly.

"Every night."

"Well, keep up the good work." The two men nodded approvingly as they settled in a booth.

Dot took their order. When she returned to the counter, she picked up the thread of her conversation with Joe. "Not a lot goes on in this town I don't hear about. Folks like to talk, and Lord knows, I'm a good listener."

"So what have you heard?" He was anxious to hear what she had to say. A lot was riding on whether or not the townspeople accepted him.

"That people are lining up on your side." She stepped down the counter and refilled a couple of coffee cups before continuing. "People see what you've done to that place of yours. How hard you've been working. They watch you and Chloe together. You can tell a lot about a man's character by how he lives, but you can tell if his heart's in the right place by how he treats his child. You have a good heart, Joe. I'm not the only one who's noticed."

He sat up straighter. "I value your opinion, Dot. If I ask you a question, will you tell me the truth?"

She leaned on the counter. "You know me, sweetie, I'm too old and too cranky to sugarcoat things. Shoot."

He grinned, knowing she would be honest. "Based on what you've heard about the election, what kind of chance do you think I have?"

She laughed and patted his arm. "Better than a one-legged man in a butt-kicking contest."

He gave her a wry look. "That good, huh?"

"Seriously? You get into the race, and you've got a good chance to win. Of course it helps that your only opponent is Richard Futterman."

"Why is that?"

"He's about as popular as a skunk at a prayer meeting."

"I don't know him. Who is he?"

"An arrogant little snot with a bad case of SMS."

"SMS?" Joe frowned. He wasn't up on modern abbreviations.

"Short Man Syndrome." Dot lowered her voice. "They don't call him Dick for nothing."

"And he's definitely running?"

"So I hear. His daddy's a rich lawyer over in Odessa which means Sonny Boy's got the money and the connections to mount a full-fledged campaign."

Joe began to doubt the sanity of his plan. What made him think he could win the election? He had no resources and no idea how to launch a successful campaign. "Doesn't sound too favorable for me, then. I don't have either one."

Dot laughed again. "Trust me. Nobody wants to see Dick Futterman become sheriff."

When Chloe finished her milkshake, Joe wiped her mouth. She smiled up at him, and he could see the future in her twinkling eyes. The old Joe may have made a lot of mistakes, but Chloe wasn't one of them. He tapped her turned-up nose playfully just to hear her laugh. They'd made a lot of progress during the past couple of weeks. He didn't feel nearly as nervous about caring for her, and she seemed to enjoy his company. She still called him Joe, but no longer asked who he was. Someday, maybe she'd think of him as Daddy, but for the time being, he'd take what he could get.

He turned to Dot. "So what you're saying is if I'm lucky, I could win by default."

"If you win, it'll be on your own merit. Once you file, get out there and talk to people. Tell 'em why you want the office. Let 'em get to know you. Show 'em how far you've come.

You always were a helluva talker, so just do what comes naturally.''

"And you think I'd make a better sheriff than this Futterman fella?'' He knew he could do the job, but no one else was aware of his past experience. He had to win votes based on what people knew about Joe.

Dot scoffed. "Are you kidding me?'' She picked up a condiment bottle. "This watered-down ketchup would make a better sheriff than Dick Futterman.'' She ruffled Chloe's hair. "Right, short stuff?''

Chloe laughed. "Right.'' She held her arms out to Joe, and he scooped her off the stool and into his lap. His heart bucked when her little arm twined around his neck. A month ago, he didn't even know she existed, and now loving this precious child was the most natural thing in the world. He might not win the election or Mallory's love. He might end up alone forever, doomed to future lives without his other half.

Being Chloe's daddy and knowing he'd be here to protect her was worth everything he'd been through.

"Glad to know I'm one step up from ketchup,'' he said wryly. "You know, Dot, you don't exactly inspire confidence in a man.''

She reached over the counter and smacked his cheek affectionately before lowering her voice. "Don't worry, Joe. Human nature being what it is, folks are bound to root for the underdog.''

Mallory was outside Saturday morning watering the flowerpots on the deck when she heard a high-pitched squeal of laughter next door. She looked across the fence and saw Chloe running around while the dog chased after her. Joe was working under one of the cottonwood trees behind the house, but she didn't have a clear view of what he was doing.

She'd spent a lot of time with the Mitchums lately. Monday through Wednesday, she baby-sat while Joe attended night classes. Brandy, busy with her paralegal coursework, had been relieved by Mallory's last progress report. Knowing father and daughter had bonded made it easier for her to be away from Chloe.

Joe had turned out to be more adept at fatherhood than Mallory would have guessed. Formerly self-absorbed and apathetic, he had surprised her by showing excellent paternal instincts. Parenting was clearly a challenge for him; he wasn't exactly a natural at playing tea party or singing along with the purple dinosaur. However, in the time he'd had Chloe, even with everything else he'd accomplished, he had made the little girl his top priority. Watching their relationship blossom had been an unexpected joy.

The more Mallory learned about Joe, the more she admired him. He'd shown amazing guts and determination. As anyone who'd ever made a New Year's resolution knew, it took real character not to backslide into old habits—not even once. As far as she knew, he hadn't stepped foot in the tavern since the accident. He no longer associated with low friends in low places, male or female. Honest and dependable, he worked hard, paid his debts and kept a clean house.

Night after night, she watched him pore over the review material, methodically memorizing the dozens of facts and equations he seemed to have forgotten from his school days. It was when she saw how hard he had to work that Mallory began to sense the depth of Joe's commitment. Maybe the forgotten knowledge was a result of the accident, but he'd had to practically relearn everything in the high school review course. To his credit, he never got frustrated. He kept at it, learning slowly but doggedly.

It wasn't so hard to make the logical extension and assume he had applied the same patient determination to other areas of his life. Hard work was something Mallory understood. She would not have gotten where she was without being equally committed to her goals. Maybe she and Joe weren't as different as she had thought.

On serious reflection, she'd shelved the pod-person theory, concluding that she'd have to be nuts to consider such a far-fetched explanation for Joe's behavior. As a doctor, she was comfortable dealing with facts, and the facts told her that Joe was indeed different. They also told her the changes she'd observed were not due to a top secret body switch, but to Joe's own obstinate efforts to *be* different.

And he was definitely different. In more ways than she could count. They had discussed the essays and short stories he read for credit during their late-night study sessions. Through them, she'd come to know him better, and he'd emerged as an even bigger enigma. She'd had no idea he held such strong opinions about integrity, honor and justice. Or where those opinions had come from. Some of his ideas were…well, old-fashioned. For example, his take on the roles of men and women in society. His declaration that males were responsible for protecting the fair sex from all unpleasantness was ironic, considering how shabbily he had treated females in the past.

She assumed his newly unearthed character was a result of his upbringing, but he balked whenever she tried to bring his late father and mother into the conversation. He said talking about them was too painful, so she didn't prod. Still, Briny thought the circumstances of Joe's father's death had played a major role in the loss of self-esteem that led to subsequent failures. She couldn't stop wondering about that part of his past.

"Docker P!" Chloe ran to the fence and yelled for Mallory's attention.

"Come and see what Joe maked me."

Smiling, she put down the hose and turned off the water. She cut across the yard and ducked between the strings of wire fencing. "What did Joe make, Chloe?"

"Come and see." The child grabbed her hand and pulled her to the old cottonwood tree where he was testing the rope swing he'd hung on a low branch.

"Ready to try 'er out, tadpole?" he asked.

"Ready!"

He lifted her onto the smooth wooden seat and told her to hold on to the ropes. He pulled the seat back gently and let go.

"Whee! This is fun! Push me higher!"

Mallory laughed. "I know how you'll be spending your spare time from now on."

"Oh, she'll get tired of it." His smile was indulgent. "She lost interest in the sandbox I made her after a couple of days."

"I still like the sandbox," Chloe called out as she swung back and forth. "But now I like the swing better."

"I've been working on my research paper." Joe nudged the swing again to keep it going. "Think you'll have time to look it over when I'm done? Correct my mistakes?"

"Sure. I'd be happy to. How about I type it up for you?"

"That would be great. My hen scratching isn't very legible. Thanks."

"No problem." Mallory stood in the shade and watched Joe play with his laughing child. Her short legs pumped, but contributed little to the movement of the swing. She was neatly dressed in hot pink shorts with a matching print top, hot pink socks and white sneakers. Mallory's heart ached with tenderness when she realized Joe had gone to the trouble of choosing a color-coordinated outfit for Chloe. His strong hands had gently brushed the little girl's shiny hair into a crooked ponytail and carefully tied her shoelaces into double knots.

She'd seen him trim the crusts off peanut butter and grape jelly sandwiches, which he then cut into quarters because that's the way Chloe liked them. He read *The Foot Book* five times in a row because Chloe asked him to. He sat on the floor for hours at a time, stacking blocks so Chloe could knock them down. He'd even taken the silly dog to the vet for shots and a bath because Chloe wanted it to sleep at the foot of her bed.

Clearly, the child had her father wrapped around her little finger.

Chloe had been less than a year old when her parents divorced. Brandy had encouraged Joe to take a more active role in their daughter's life, but it seemed he couldn't be bothered. If her assessment was true, then the bolt of lightning that had knocked Joe off the utility pole had given Chloe a special gift, one that would have a powerful and positive impact on her life.

The gift of a loving and caring father.

Mallory couldn't help thinking that she too had been given a gift the day she'd saved Joe. Sometimes it unnerved her to think that if she hadn't been in the right place at just the right time, he'd be gone from the world forever. She never would have gotten to know how wonderful the man she'd previously discounted could be. Whether because of the near-death experience, or having merely had his eyes opened to his mistakes, he'd changed.

In doing so, he'd also changed her without even realizing it. Knowing him had made her feel strangely complete, less satisfied with her solitary life. It was as if she'd been sleepwalking, afraid to wake up, afraid to live. Healing others was a noble profession. Accepting others was even more so.

Regardless of what happened between her and Joe Mitchum, Mallory knew she would never be the same again.

"Watch me, Docker P!"

"I'm watching, Chloe. Hold on tight."

"Joe won't let me fall," the child declared confidently.

But he'd let Mallory fall. She met his gaze and a surge of raw emotion filled her until it threatened to overcome her. This mystery man had done nothing but antagonize her for years; now she only felt at peace when he was near. When they were apart, it was as though a vital part of herself was missing. For weeks, she'd fought the impossible. She'd tried to convince herself that what she felt could not be real.

She couldn't possibly fall in love with Joe Mitchum.

And yet, somehow in the process of restarting his heart she'd given him hers.

Chapter Eleven

A week later, as Mallory left the last study session before Joe's final exam, he handed her a sheaf of notebook paper. He'd been nervous about taking the tests, so they'd put in extra hours reviewing tonight, drilling on the material until he could answer the questions in his sleep.

She glanced at the handwritten sheets. "What's this?"

"You offered to look over my research paper for mistakes. Remember?"

"Oh, right. Since you don't have a computer, I'll type it for you."

"Thanks. Typing is worth extra points."

"Sure. No problem. I'll get it to you as soon as I can." She tried to read the title page, but he reclaimed the papers and folded them in half.

"Look at it later." He tucked the sheets under her arm. When she reached for the doorknob, he braced his hand on the jamb beside her head. "Before you go, I want you to know I never would've gotten this far without you."

She waved off any contribution she might have made. "Nonsense. You would have done just fine on your own. You're a quick study and won't have any trouble on the tests."

He tipped his head down until his forehead almost touched hers. His eyes and smile were hopeful. "Do you really believe in me?"

More than she had ever thought possible. "I do believe in you, Joe." He was too close. She stepped back when she felt her skin yearning toward him, seeking his touch. For days now, she had longed for the amazing feelings to fill her up again, to crowd out the doubts that haunted her. Maybe, if she gave him a friendly, good-night kiss, she would smell the phantom roses.

Did she dare? She'd missed the pleasing fragrance. It gave her a sense of well-being that filled all the empty places in her soul. Instead of frightening her, the prospect of the odd sensation was strangely comforting.

Denied too long, need welled up within her. She'd been strong when they studied together, matching self-control and willpower against hormones and desire. Despite the urgent messages her body fired into her brain, she had managed to maintain a tenuous emotional distance between herself and Joe.

She had resolved to play it safe until the day he built the swing and she realized she was dangerously close to losing her heart. She had to be careful. Accepting that she *might* have a future with Joe Mitchum was all she could handle. Acting on errant physical impulses was out of the question.

That is, unless her libido managed to override her common sense again.

He leaned closer, his lips a breath away from hers. "It means a lot to know I have your faith."

She edged away. "Have faith in yourself. That's what counts. You didn't do this for me."

"Everything I do is for you," he contradicted.

"Don't say that."

"It's true. You're my reason for living. The only reason I'm here." His words took on a note of desperation. "Why can't you believe in us?"

"Joe, please."

He cupped her face in both hands and turned it up. "I always oblige a lady.'' His lips lowered onto hers, igniting a series of wondrous sensations. Her eyes closed as the heat of his mouth spread through her like thermal radiation, building until she worried about spontaneous combustion. Layered over the heat was the powerful and very real scent of old-fashioned roses. It flooded through her, filling her senses with sweet, liquid nectar. He deepened the kiss, but the hungry caress only supercharged her with a shock of color.

Yellow.

Yellow roses. A whole bouquet of them.

She'd never experienced a visual hallucination before, if that's what it was. Other than the scent of roses, the feelings evoked by Joe's touch had been as vague as dreams forgotten in the light of day. This was sensory overload. Joe pulled her close, and with the contact came another vision. Or was it a memory? She couldn't decide. She couldn't even breathe.

A man on one knee. A proposal? Her eyes were shut, and yet she saw him clearly. Sunlight shimmered behind him, obscuring his face and glinting off the silver ring he slid on her finger.

Impossible. How could she remember an event that had never happened? How could she feel the weight of a thin, diamond-studded band when it had never existed? It wasn't real. None of this was real.

She opened her eyes and broke the kiss, then pulled herself out of Joe's embrace. ''What's going on here?''

He smiled and tenderly hooked a stray strand of hair behind her ear. ''I was just kissing my girl good-night. Anything wrong with that?''

When he moved to pick up where he'd left off, she backed into the living room. ''What do you know about roses?'' She was careful to keep her voice down so she wouldn't awaken Chloe.

Startled by her question, he quickly masked his expression. ''Roses won't be on the test, will they?''

''Stop stonewalling me, Joe.'' It was hard to make demands in a whisper. ''Tell me about roses.''

He shrugged. ''Big flower. Nice smell. Sharp thorns.''

"Yellow roses," she insisted.

"'The Yellow Rose of Texas' is a song, isn't it? I don't remember how it goes exactly, but it's something like this." He cleared his throat and sung in a husky baritone. "The yellow rose of Texas will be mine forever more."

"Stop it! I'm not talking about a song." She buried her face in her hands while she collected her thoughts, and then raked them through her hair in frustration. "Strange things happen when you kiss me."

"Strange bad? Or strange good?"

"I don't know. *Strange*. It's like I'm being transported to another place. Another time. How do you explain that?"

He grinned. "I must be a helluva lot better kisser than I thought."

"Be serious. I want to pretend the feelings aren't real, but they are. I just had some crazy Technicolor déjà vu moment or whatever you want to call it."

"So?"

"So, before I was just smelling flowers. Now I'm seeing things. I'm a doctor remember? Distorted sensory perceptions are not normal."

"What do you think it means?" he asked cautiously.

"Well, I'm either having a psychotic episode, which is unlikely. Or some kind of brain tumor is short-circuiting my neurons."

"You don't have a tumor," he said quietly.

"So what's wrong with me? Why am I seeing a man with a bouquet of yellow roses?"

"Did you recognize him?"

"I couldn't see his face, but I think he was asking me to marry him. I actually felt him slip the ring on my finger."

"And...you feel this ring now?"

She huffed out a frustrated sigh. She recognized that tone. It was the same one she used with known hypochondriacs when asking about their nonexistent ills. "No! I don't feel it now! It only happens when you kiss me."

He stepped closer. "I think we need to put those odd feelings of yours to the test."

She stepped back and eyed him with suspicion. "What kind of test?"

"I think we should keep kissing until they go away." He reached for her, but she sidestepped him and headed for the door.

"Great idea! That would be like recommending I keep hitting my thumb with a hammer until it stops hurting. No thank you."

"You're comparing kissing me with pounding your thumb?" He tried to look hurt, but he was a terrible actor. Amusement sparkled in his warm eyes.

"This is not funny. You know more than you're telling me. Why won't you talk to me about this?"

His amusement vanished, replaced by an unreadable expression. He started to speak, hesitated, then finally said, "I wish I could tell you what you want to hear, Mallory. Unfortunately, there is nothing I can say."

She stalked past him and stopped at the door. "Then there's nothing for me to say either. I'll type your paper and leave it under the welcome mat. Good luck on your test, Joe. Goodbye."

"Mallory!" He followed her outside, but she bolted off the porch and headed for home. "Wait."

She didn't slow down to answer. When she reached the safety of her own back door, she turned and looked back. Joe stood where she'd left him. He was silhouetted in the silver glow of the full moon, his face obscured by shadows. Her stomach turned over and her heart pounded.

He looked just like the man in her vision.

Joe watched Mallory disappear into her house. It killed him to know how much his evasions had hurt her. He'd barely conquered his desire to blurt out the truth. Only the threat of the high price he'd pay for his honesty had kept him silent. Celestian had made it clear that breaking the rule of silence would have serious consequences. If he told her anything, he could be recalled, ruining their only chance to be together. Not that she would ever believe they had an eternal connection.

His heart had nearly stopped when she told him about the roses and the ring. He knew he was the man in her vision, but his own memories had faded during his time as Joe, and the details were no longer sharp in his mind. He did remember the yellow roses. They'd been her favorite flowers, and he'd given her the biggest bunch he could find the night he asked her to be his wife. He'd gone down on one knee, called her his Yellow Rose, and promised to spend the rest of his life making her happy.

He couldn't have known one life would not be enough.

He went inside and sank into a kitchen chair. Some moments just called for a drink, but he'd sworn not to have alcohol in the house. The old Joe had misused it, and he didn't want to take the risk. Still, a shot of tarantula juice would go a long way toward making him feel better about lying to Mallory.

He hadn't wanted to be untruthful, but there was probably a good reason for the no-tell rule. The idea of a lonely spirit walking into another man's life would be a pretty big helping for anyone to swallow, especially someone as sensible and down-to-earth as Mallory. He'd been so excited about returning, he hadn't considered all the obstacles he would face. When he'd awakened in the hospital, he'd thought the hardest part was over, that happily ever after was guaranteed.

He never imagined convincing Mallory to love him would be so hard.

Joe made a special trip into town to turn in the research paper Mallory had carefully typed and left in a large envelope on his front porch. She had avoided him since the rose incident, but on the evening of his exam, she showed up without question to stay with Chloe. She said nothing about the visions or the unspoken and unexplainable ties that bound them together. Again, she wished him good luck before letting herself be distracted by the picture book Chloe asked her to read.

Thanks to Mallory's diligent tutoring, Joe completed the high school review exam in the allotted time. He had no idea what kind of grade he might have made, but all he had to do was pass. Surely, he had gotten sixty percent of the questions right. The English test was harder, and he struggled with an essay question requiring him to contrast and compare the works of nineteenth-century American poets. He'd never understood poetry, and feared that even with Mallory's coaching, he wouldn't get full credit. If he didn't pass the English course, the rest wouldn't matter. He wouldn't get his GED. He'd miss the deadline to file for the election. He'd lose his shot at being sheriff.

He'd have to continue being a handyman. He wouldn't ask Mallory to marry him with no more to offer than that.

The teacher returned his research paper at the end of the class period. Joe's breath caught when he saw a red A+ with the comment that she'd found his conclusions particularly insightful. If he'd done half as well on the rest of the test, everything would be all right.

He whistled as he crossed the parking lot. At least he had the good news of the A+ to balance the trepidation of unknown test scores. Knowing the teacher wouldn't post grades until the next afternoon would make for a long night. His optimism vanished with a groan when he reached his truck and found Glorieta Tadlock waiting for him. He'd thought the woman was out of his life forever. No such luck.

"Hey there, Miss Tadlock. How're you doing this evening?"

"Miss Tadlock?" she scoffed. "Pretty formal, aren't we?" She leaned into him, and he couldn't tell which was more unappealing: the cloying smell of her perfume or the beer on her breath. "You used to call me Glori."

"In case you haven't noticed, I stopped doing a lot of things I used to do."

"I don't want to be one of the things you stop doing." She laughed and planted herself square in front of him, so close that her bosom, revealed by a low-necked blouse, nearly touched his chest. "C'mon, Joe. We had some fun together. I've got a six-pack of tallboys in the car. Part of one anyway. Why don't you come over to my place? We can party just like old times."

"Thanks for the invite, Miss Tadlock, but I can't take you up on it." He reached for the door handle. "I have to get home to my little girl."

"I can't believe you're turning me down." She pouted and kicked the truck door. "It's that doctor, isn't it?"

"What?"

"Do you seriously think someone like Mallory Peterson would give a guy like you the time of day?"

He refused to discuss Mallory with her and moved to open the door. "I'm going now." He started the engine, but couldn't back out of the parking space because Glorieta stuck her frowzy blond head in the open window.

"You're kidding yourself, Joe Mitchum, if you think you mean anything to that woman. You're just another one of her community projects. Miss Perfect likes to help the underprivileged, you know. She's so high-and-mighty, it's a wonder she doesn't get a nosebleed."

Her words were slurred, but they sent an arrow of doubt straight into his heart. *Was* he kidding himself? Would Mallory ever love him? If not, everything he'd done in this life had been pointless. His existence was pointless. "I think you need to go home, Miss Tadlock, and sleep it off."

"You want me to drive?" She jingled her car keys in his face. "Hey, I'm under the influence. I'm a danger to myself and unsuspecting motorists." She swayed on her feet, and he realized she was as tipsy as a peach-orchard sow. "Don't you watch TV, Joe? Friends don't let friends drive drunk."

Frustration and anger warred with his sense of duty. Time was precious, and he didn't care to waste a minute of it on this persistent pest. All he wanted to do was get home so he could talk to Mallory. He was still bound by the rule of silence, but he couldn't bear to have things so unresolved between them.

Yet he couldn't let this fool woman drive.

"C'mon, Joe. Be a hero. Take me home."

He sighed. Gallantry definitely had it drawbacks. "Get in."

Giggling, she grabbed the beer out of her car and ran around the front of the truck. She climbed in beside him and scooted way too close for comfort. Her head dropped onto his shoulder. "I'm really feeling woozy, honey. You might have to tuck me into bed."

Mallory glanced at her watch and realized Joe was much later than usual. Either the tests had run over, or he'd waited while the teacher scored them. She tiptoed into the bedroom to check on Chloe. A beam of moonlight slanted across the bed, and the dog raised his head to let her know he was on duty. "Good boy, Celestian," she whispered. "Keep the monsters away."

Chloe was sprawled in the rumpled bed, her tiny arms and legs tangled in the sheet. Mallory straightened the covers, and the little girl stirred.

"Joe?" she murmured.

"No, honey. Daddy's not home yet. Go back to sleep."

Chloe would be leaving soon. The last time they spoke, Brandy said she missed Chloe and was coming after her Saturday. The single mother was pleased that Joe now wanted to take advantage of the visitation agreement and was willing to have his daughter every other weekend and alternating holidays in the future.

Mallory was glad Brandy had given Joe a second chance. The child needed her father, and he needed her. Somehow, he'd managed to make up for three years of neglect in less than four weeks.

She went into the kitchen for a glass of water. Where was he? She was a little anxious to hear how the tests had gone. He'd studied so hard; he'd be disappointed if he didn't pass. Without a GED, he had no hope of getting into the election because he'd miss the deadline for filing. She didn't understand why he was determined to run, but like so many Joe-related subjects, she'd given up trying to figure it out.

She dozed on the sofa, waking when she heard him come in. Glancing at the time, she saw that it was after midnight.

"Sorry I'm late," he apologized.

She yawned. "Surely the test didn't take this long?"

"No. I got…sidetracked in town. I didn't mean to keep you up so late."

"No problem, but I need to get home. I have work tomorrow." As she passed him on her way to the door, she caught a whiff of a familiar scent. No roses this time. She inhaled deeply to make sure. Her nostrils quivered. Joe smelled like perfume, the cheap kind purchased in drugstores. He also smelled like beer. In fact, he positively reeked of it.

Her first impulse was to demand to know where he'd been the past three hours, but what he did was none of her business. He was a free agent and didn't owe her an explanation. If he wanted to celebrate with someone who bought perfume in quart bottles, he didn't have to justify his actions to her.

Sick disappointment settled in the pit of her stomach. She'd thought his days of being a country song cliché were over. It hurt to think he'd been unable to resist the temptation of his old lifestyle after all. Willing women and cold beer. Two steps backward in the self-improvement game.

"Good night, Joe." Scalding tears welled behind her eyes, and she blinked them back. She had to get out before he saw how upset she was. She wouldn't cry. He couldn't make her cry.

"Don't you want to hear about the test?" he asked hopefully.

"Not tonight. It's late. I have to go." She had another vision, but there was nothing unexplainable about this one. She shook her head to rid herself of the hateful picture. She didn't want to think about Joe in the arms of a woman like those who hung out at Whiskey Pete's. An easy-to-please woman, one who didn't try to hold him up to impossible standards. One who wanted him for what he was, what he'd always been. A fun-loving liar.

"I got an A+ on my research assignment."

"Congratulations." She forced the words out around the lump in her throat. "You did a good job. You deserved high marks." Under different circumstances, she would have stayed and discussed his paper, which had been well researched and thought provoking. She'd enjoyed reading his observations as she'd typed them, thinking he'd written so knowledgeably on the subject, it was almost as if he had firsthand experience.

Which was ridiculous. No way could he have firsthand experience on that particular topic. The title of his paper was "A Nineteenth Century Man in The Twenty-First Century: Changes in American Culture in the Last One Hundred Years."

With her chest tight and aching, Mallory bolted before he could say anything else. She couldn't bear to hear his lies or be reminded of how closely she'd come to letting him break her heart. With only the pale half-moon to witness her misery, she ran through the darkness toward her cold, empty house.

Chapter Twelve

"Psst, Joe. Wake up. We have to talk."

Startled from deep sleep a few nights later, Joe rubbed his eyes and looked around. The empty bedroom was quiet. Dark. Lit only by a thin blade of moonlight knifing through half-drawn drapes. Had the familiar voice spoken to him in a dream?

The dog usually slept with Chloe, but tonight it sat at the foot of Joe's bed with its head cocked to one side. "We have a little problem."

Joe scrambled back against the headboard. Why the hell did Celestian the dog suddenly sound like Celestian the time-out monitor? He *had* to be dreaming. "What the—?"

"Look, we don't have time to go through the whole 'Oh-my-goodness-a-talking dog' routine. I'll be in even bigger trouble if You-Know-Who finds out I'm doing this."

Joe switched on the bedside lamp for a better look. Despite his shocking new verbal skills, the little white mongrel didn't look any different—still dumb as a bag of marbles. "I'm dreaming."

"No, you're not. We don't have time for that either. I'm here, and we need to talk about our problem."

He squinted, peering at the dog. "Is that you, Celestian?"

"Of course, it's me."

"Dogs can't talk."

The animal heaved a very human sigh. "We can do things, all right? Think of it this way, the canine isn't really talking. It's an amplifier. A flesh-and-blood woofer, if you will. Desperate situations call for desperate measures."

Joe shook his head. This middle of the night visit was beyond bizarre, but compared to the big picture, what was a talking dog, more or less? "Spit it out. What's the problem?"

"The old Joe wants his body back."

"What?" He angled up and sat on the edge of the bed.

"There was a...slight glitch when he alighted. He found out about it. Now he's squawking about exercising his spirit rights. What a crybaby!"

"Sorry, buddy, you lost me."

The dog picked its way over the rumpled bedcovers and sat beside Joe, placing a paw on his bare leg. When he looked up and panted, the voice of Joe's old nemesis rolled out of his mouth. "There are rules. Complex rules you don't need to know about. Suffice to say, when the original Joe vacated his mortal coil, I...well, I guess I acted impulsively."

A lump of dread dropped to the bottom of Joe's stomach. "What did you do?"

"I sort of failed to inform him of his rights."

"What rights?"

The dog cocked his head in the opposite direction, and Celestian reeled off the rule by rote. "An alighted spirit retains first reentry privileges should the coil in question be resuscitated."

Joe frowned in confusion. "But I thought he chose to get in line for a new assignment hoping to be dealt a better hand the next time around?"

The dog panted, and its pink tongue lolled out. "That may have been what I told you. I was so excited at the prospect of booting you from time-out that I...uh...might have embroidered the truth."

"You mean you lied?" Joe raked his hair in frustration.

"It was a sin of omission, but never mind that. When the old Joe saw how well he was doing down here, he demanded to reclaim his body."

Joe jumped up and paced the room in his skivvies. "What do you mean how well *he's* doing? I'm the one who turned his sorry life around."

"But you *are* Joe Mitchum now. You've elevated his mortal coil from a dissolute, and dare we say pointless, existence to one with a future. Well done, by the way. Joe's prospects are better than he ever thought they could be. The good doctor is in love with him—"

"Him?" Joe whirled around. "You mean me!"

"Don't get bogged down in complicated semantics. All right, Mallory Peterson is in love with you, then."

"She is?" Hope chipped away at the boulder of dread. "How do you know? She hasn't said a word. She won't even talk to me."

"Pay attention. We can do things. We know things. It has been duly noted that you've gotten Joe out of debt, repaired all his broken relationships, given him a decent place to live and a future worth living. You've restored his self-confidence, given him back his self-respect and earned him the esteem of everyone in town. Now that he's going to be the new sheriff—"

"He is? You mean, *I* am?" He stopped pacing and looked down at the dog hunkered on his bed. "Wait. I just filed the Declaration of Candidacy yesterday. They haven't even held the runoffs yet, so how can you—"

"What part of 'We know things' did you not understand? Come on. Stay with me here. I only have a short break before I have to return to work."

"I can't believe this." He sank to the edge of the bed again, propping his head in his hands. Despair had replaced dread. He was doomed. Despite popular belief, you *could* argue with City Hall. But you sure as shootin' couldn't argue with the After Place. "The old Joe wants *my* life back!"

"Most of it. Actually, I don't think he's too keen on

sobriety, monogamy or fatherhood, but he thinks if he can get Mallory Peterson, he can have any woman he wants.''

"Mallory doesn't care about him. Whatever feelings she has are for me, not Joe Mitchum! None of this would have happened if he'd returned to his mortal coil after the lightning strike.''

The dog stretched out on the bed beside him. "You're preaching to the choir, pal. I've been fully apprised of that little detail. Nonetheless, he wants to come back, and because of a technicality, he's entitled.''

"And you're going to let me get evicted?"

"It's out of my hands. In fact, I've been busted down to sorting prayers in Receiving. I'm taking a big chance even speaking to you like this.''

"So what's going to happen?" He didn't want to know, but not knowing was far worse.

"I can't say. I'm out of the loop now. The matter has been turned over to the Department of Natural Forces. I suspect they'll create a diversion during which another switch can be made.''

"So I'll alight, and the old Joe will take possession of the coil?"

The dog scratched his ear. "Something like that.''

"What will happen to me?" He stared out the window and watched as the first blood red fingers of dawn crawled over the horizon. Another day gone. One less chance to win Mallory's respect and affection. Lost.

"Life is everlasting. Once you alight in Reception for recycling, you'll get a new start in a new life. That's not so bad, is it?"

He banged his fist down on the bed, making the little dog bounce. "I don't want another new start. I just had one. And if you really want to know, it was pure hell there for awhile.''

The dog whimpered and jumped off the bed. "Don't say that word.''

"I'm starting to feel like the pea in a shell game. What'll it be next? Will they strike me down with another lightning bolt and send in the replacement?"

"They'll have to be a little more original than that. They've already used lightning twice. A third time would be stretching credibility."

His gaze snapped to Celestian. "You mean the old Joe getting struck was planned? It wasn't just an accident?"

The dog sidled onto his lap. "Have you not been paying attention? There *are* no accidents."

Understanding dawned along with the new day streaking the sky. "So I was meant to come back all along? I was meant to have a second chance with Mallory. It was in The Plan for me to redeem Joe's honor and restore Chloe's faith in her father. Is that what you're telling me?"

"Well, yes, but I didn't know that at the time. I sincerely believed I needed to intercede to get you back down here."

"So when you jumped the gun you created the noose to hang me with."

"It's really more of a loophole. And if it's any consolation, I genuinely regret taking matters into my own hands. Given the choice, the old Joe would have chosen to vacate and everything would have worked out as planned."

"And I wouldn't have to go back."

The dog rooted his way under the covers, knowing he was in trouble. He raised his blanket-draped head and held Joe's gaze. "What's done is done. Life goes on. It's always darkest before the dawn. Every cloud has a silver lining."

Joe snatched off the blanket, sending the dog scurrying to the far end of the bed. "Stop spouting idiotic clichés. They don't make me feel any better! Do you know what you've done?"

"I said I was sorry." Celestian acted like the wronged party. "I didn't have to tell you. The switch could have just happened, and you never would have known why. I'm trying to help."

"Well, stop. I don't think I can't stand any more of your brand of help."

The dog crawled forward cautiously and rested its head on Joe's leg. It looked up, its dark eyes liquid with remorse. "I really am sorry."

"Is there nothing I can do? No way out of this nightmare? I can't go back now. I love Mallory. I love Chloe. I have a future, and I don't want to lose it." He reached down and grasped the dog's head between his hands. "Tell me there's something I can do."

Celestian whined. "I swore not to interfere again."

"Now is not a good time to go on the wagon. If there's any hope of fixing this mess you've created, you'd better spit it out!"

"You do know it's not the dog's fault, right?"

"Yes! Dammit! What can I do?"

"I'm going to regret telling you this."

"You'll regret not telling me, because I won't come back if I can't be with Mallory. When I alight in that big white place, I plan to stay forever, doing everything I can to make a total misery of your eternity."

The dog whimpered before Celestian's words tumbled out in one frightened breath. "In order for you to stay Mallory has to swear her undying love and agree to spend the rest of her life with you."

Relief evaporated Joe's anger just as the morning sun would evaporate the dew. "That's all?"

"That's not enough?"

"You already said she loves me."

"*She* has to say she loves you. Mallory Peterson is a nervous Nelly. She's been afraid to trust her feelings ever since your Will Pendleton died and left her Molly Earnshaw all alone over a hundred years ago. She certainly doesn't trust Joe now. Getting her to actually say the words could be extremely difficult."

"How much time do I have?"

"That's the problem. I have no idea. The matter is out of my hands. Who knows what those guys in Natural Forces will come up with? It could be tomorrow. Or next week. Even next year. Time is irrelevant, you know."

"Not to me." With his heart pounding in his chest, Joe crossed to the window and watched the rising sun burn across the landscape. "Time is the measure of life, and I've run out of it."

The next morning, Joe stacked dirty dishes in the sink and thought about what Celestian had said. He was lost for good unless Mallory professed her love for him, and soon. That shocking news and Chloe's imminent departure conspired to ruin his day. Chloe wasn't happy about leaving and had moped through breakfast. Even Joe's flapjack-flipping tricks had failed to put a smile on her face.

"C'mon tadpole. Time to pack." She helped him pick up the toys scattered around the room that would be hers, at least every other weekend and alternating holidays. Wordlessly, they decided which dolls and books to stow in boxes for the trip back to Brandy's parents' home and which ones would stay.

"Do I hafta go?" She handed Joe a floppy blue bunny, which he placed gently on top of the "go" pile.

"Don't you want to see Mommy?"

"Yes. But I don't want to leave you."

He didn't want to leave her either. If he did, he wouldn't be coming back. Ever. Worried that like a dog or a horse, the child could sense his fear, he pasted on a fake smile. "I'll pick you up next weekend. We'll have regular visits from here on out." He hoped he wasn't lying. The old Joe had better do right by her, or…what? What could he do? Nothing. He burned with impotent rage at the injustice. The old Joe didn't deserve Chloe or Mallory.

"I know." Her bottom lip quivered.

"So what's wrong?" He collected bright-colored hair ribbons from the top of the dresser and dropped them into her suitcase.

She removed the bunny from the "go" pile and propped it against the pillow on the bed. "You'll be sad."

"True enough. I'll miss you." He couldn't believe how much. In a few short weeks, the child had found a forever home in his heart. He smiled again to reassure her. "The week will go fast. We'll have fun next time you visit. You can help me campaign for sheriff.'' If the old Joe returned before the election, would he work hard enough to win? What kind of sheriff would he be? Would he tear down everything Joe had built in his absence?

She sat on the floor, and the little dog jumped into her lap. She hugged him, and a fallen tear dampened his white fur. ''I'll miss you *and* my doggie.''

''He'll be here with his tail wagging when you come back.'' Joe sat on the bed, his heart bursting with tender feelings for the girl. Of all the good things he'd accomplished since waking up in Joe's life, Chloe was the best.

''If I go home, you won't have nobody to make you smile.''

''I just have to think about you, darlin.' That's all it takes.''

She slipped out from under the dog and ran to him. Climbing into his lap, she clung to his neck, squeezing with all the strength her tiny arms possessed. ''I love you a whole much, Joe.''

His filled-up heart turned over as he hugged her back. ''I love you, too.''

She pressed her face close to his and whispered in his ear. ''I know you're not him, but will you stay here forever?''

Forever? He couldn't make that promise. Even tomorrow was uncertain. He could be called away by the next big wind or flash flood. He struggled for words that weren't a lie. ''You'll always be my little girl.''

She kissed his cheek. ''Will you always be my Daddy?''

Daddy. Why hadn't Celestian just cut the heart right out of him? It wouldn't have hurt this much. ''A herd of wild broncos couldn't drag me away from you, tadpole.'' Only fate could do that. He held her close. The bubblegum scent of the bubbles she poured in her bathwater filled his nostrils and stung his eyes, filling them with tears.

Mallory tossed a hastily packed overnight bag into the front seat of her truck. She had to get away. Joe lived so close she could feel his presence everywhere. Every time she looked out the window, she saw the former eyesore he had transformed into a welcoming home. When the swing he'd made his little

girl rustled in the wind, it reminded her of the family he'd
created. During the day, the roar of his lawn mower told her
he was near. When the quiet nights came, even the insects
chirping in the grass seemed to chant his name.

Joe. Joe. Joe.

When had he become so important to her? She never should
have let her feelings get so out of hand. She'd lost control,
when control was what she valued most. Been illogical when
only logic was safe. She'd come close to playing the fool by
wanting to believe in him so badly that she'd let herself be
deceived by appearances.

As an afterthought, she checked her flowers, finding them
parched in the July heat. Her drooping spirits were as wilted
as the petunias, crushed by the evidence of Joe's backsliding.
She turned on the hose and a rush of life-giving water poured
forth. The thirsty plants would be quickly renewed. All she
had to do was soak the pots. Too bad her faith in Joe could
not be as easily revived. Twist a spigot and wash the doubts
away. If only it were that simple.

When she decided to take an impromptu trip, she'd called
Brindon and Dorian, hoping they would be in Dallas for the
weekend. Dorian was flying to Oklahoma City to host a foundation fund-raiser, but Briny planned to spend the weekend at
the Burrell ranch outside Fort Worth checking operations. He
said he'd be glad to have company if she wanted to meet him
there.

She had gratefully accepted the invitation. If anyone could
help her put things into perspective, it was Briny. He was the
only one who really knew Joe, the man at the eye of her
emotional storm. She hadn't spoken to him since he'd taken
the GED test, but she'd heard he passed with points to spare.
The ever-active Slapdown grapevine had also filled her in on
the details of what had detained him in town that night.

A patient who lived across the street from Glorieta Tadlock
reported seeing Joe come home with the woman that night and
walk her to the door. In her words "Glorieta was wrapped
around Joe tighter than a hatband." That news only confirmed
suspicions aroused by the lingering scent of eau de tramp. The

neighbor hadn't seen Joe leave Glorieta's, but three hours were unaccounted for between the end of his test and the time he showed up at home.

Three hours were long enough.

Surprisingly, Mallory couldn't work up enough steam to be angry with him. He'd put his place to rights. He'd completed his education. Filed for the election. There was no question he'd become the father Chloe needed. He'd accomplished a lot in a short time. It was probably asking too much for him to put drinking and womanizing behind him, too. As her father often said, a bobcat might change some of its spots, but it couldn't change them all.

While she wasn't mad at Joe, she was furious with herself. She'd been naive enough to think a man could overcome twelve years of bad habits in a couple of months. She'd wanted to believe in him. If Joe Mitchum could pull himself out of the dreadful mire of his life, there was hope for everyone. Without knowing it, he had strengthened her faith in mankind, and then destroyed that faith with one careless act.

"Mallory?"

She whirled around and fumbled with the hose. Anticipation and trepidation cranked up her heart rate as Joe walked toward her. Tall and lean in his white hat and boots, he was as strong and straight as an old-time Western hero. In knife-creased jeans and crisp white shirt, he definitely looked the part. She'd let his bigger-than-life exterior blind her to the fact that at heart he was just an ordinary man with intolerable weaknesses and a long history of hurting those who cared about him.

"I heard you passed the test and filed for the election. Congratulations." She focused on spraying water into the flowerpots. She was afraid to look at him again. Afraid to see the shadows of an impossible past in his eyes. She couldn't afford to believe in him again. Her heart couldn't take it.

"I owe it all to you." He smiled and removed his hat, a sweetly old-fashioned gesture. Glancing in the truck, he saw her bag. "Going somewhere?"

"Actually, I'm on my way out of town for the weekend."

"So you won't be around?" His smile faded into sadness. "Brandy came for Chloe."

"But she'll be back next weekend, right?"

"Right." His uncertainty tightened around the word, reached out to her. Pulled her with hidden meaning, like a puzzle she couldn't quite figure out. "Before she left, Chloe called me Daddy."

So he'd passed more than one test. If Mallory had any doubts, Joe's earnest expression convinced her that he really did love his daughter. It obviously meant a lot to him to know he'd finally proven himself to the child. Restored her trust in him. But then, little girls were forgiving. So much more willing to risk their hearts than big girls. They didn't question motives or sincerity. They didn't let unanswered questions tear them apart. Bittersweet yearning poured through Mallory. If only she could view life through a child's innocent eyes. With vision unclouded by cynicism and doubt.

With a heart open to love.

"I came to ask you to do me the honor of having dinner tonight. Could you change your plans?"

"I don't think so, Joe." Mallory steeled herself against his words and the sharp desperation that pried at the edges of her resolve.

"You've been making yourself mighty scarce lately." He stood with his hat in his hand. A familiar stranger.

"I've been busy." Busy trying not to think of him. Trying harder not to think of him with Glorieta Tadlock.

"If you're willing, I'd sure like us to spend more time together."

"No, Joe. I'm not willing." She turned off the spigot and wound the hose on the reel. "I need to get on the road. Is there something you want?"

He leaned against the driver-side door so she couldn't make her escape.

"I want us to be together. To get past whatever is standing between us."

He was so close she could smell the coffee he'd had for breakfast. She longed for the shelter of his strong arms, but knew the contact was too dangerous. She had to get out of here. She couldn't stop and smell the roses today. She couldn't risk recalling memories that didn't exist. "Get out of my way, Joe. Let me go."

"How can I let you go when I love you so much? Dang it, Mallory, this isn't how I wanted to tell you." He held her upper arms, forcing her to look at him. "I wanted to court you proper before I proposed."

Joe couldn't love her. She wouldn't let him. "Court me?" she asked incredulously. "What makes you think I want to be *courted?* By you or anyone else? Don't waste your breath proposing."

"Why are you so angry?" he beseeched. "Don't leave me like this, Mallory. We may not have another chance."

His desolation stunned her. When she looked deeply into his troubled brown eyes, she saw unbearable sorrow in their depths. He pulled her into his arms. Held her, pressed his lips to hers, kissed her like a condemned man making his last kiss count. Filled with memories that couldn't possibly belong to her, Mallory tore herself from Joe's embrace and climbed into her truck.

"Mallory! Don't leave me."

The sobs started before she reached the road. Joe had changed. She was the one who hadn't.

She still couldn't trust. Not him. Not herself.

And not in love.

Chapter Thirteen

That evening over a quiet dinner in the Burrell Ranch kitchen, Mallory and Brindon talked about the baby he and his wife were expecting. She answered his concerns regarding Dorian's physical changes and discussed how a child would alter their lives. Since the topic of change had been opened, Mallory turned the conversation to Joe's recent accomplishments. Briny agreed his friend had indeed undergone an incredible transformation since his accident.

When they finished eating, the housekeeper came in to clear the table. They retired to the comfortable Spanish-style den where Mallory admired Prudence Burrell's extensive collection of Native American pottery. Joe's last words echoed through her mind.

Mallory, don't leave me.

Briny was onto her delaying tactics. As soon as she sat on the oversize leather sofa, he dropped into the massive chair opposite her and leaned back, propping one booted foot on his knee. "Okay, Mal. Time to stop beating around the bush and talk about what's really on your mind."

His directness didn't surprise her. He knew her too well to let her get away with anything. "Am I that transparent?"

He grinned. "You didn't drive all the way out here for chit-chat. What's going on?"

"I don't know," she admitted. "But whatever it is, it's not…normal."

He reminded her that not too long ago, she had helped him make sense of his conflicted feelings. He'd be happy to return the favor if she'd let him. Since he was one of the least judgmental people she knew, Mallory took the plunge and described the odd sensory phenomenon that freaked her out whenever she was with Joe.

His brows rose when she mentioned the Technicolor visions and roses and the ring that wasn't real, but he encouraged her to continue. She told him about all the things Joe didn't know but should. Then she told him about Joe's research paper, which made her believe he knew things he shouldn't.

Relieved to finally have someone who really listened, she talked all around the subject. It took Briny's gentle urging to make her finally admit that the feelings she had for Joe were as strong as they were impossible to explain.

"You're my best friend," she said. "Tell me I'm not losing my mind."

He rose and gave her a brotherly hug. "You're not losing your mind, honey. You're in love."

"That's what I'm afraid of." She shook her head. Admitting the depth of her feelings for Joe was harder than she thought. "Help me find a rational explanation for what's happening."

"Well, that might be a problem." Briny grinned as he returned to his chair. "Love is illogical. For some people, the earth moves. Others hear bells." He smiled. "I'll admit smelling roses is a little outside the box, but then you've never been ordinary."

She disagreed. "The earth moving and bells ringing are metaphors. They're not real."

"That's true. We use love as a metaphor to sell everything from cars to macaroni and cheese. As a concept, it inspires art, literature and war. The abstract idea we call love only becomes real when we meet the right person."

Her eyes narrowed. "When did you become so philosophical?"

"I have more time to read now," he teased. "Trust me, Mal, when you meet the person you're meant to be with, feelings are heightened. Sounds become more beautiful. Colors are suddenly brighter."

"I don't know." His explanation seemed too simplistic to account for anything as neurologically complicated as visions. "There's more to it than that."

He leaned forward, his forearms resting on his thighs. "You're an intelligent woman. You make a living figuring out what's wrong with people so you can fix them. For once, don't get hung up trying to be logical. You can't explain love, but if you're smart, you accept it when it comes into your life."

She sighed. She was getting nowhere. If she had a better understanding of the events that had shaped Joe's past, she might gain the insight she needed. "Tell me what happened to Joe. Why did he drop out of life?"

Briny shrugged. "All I know is what he's told me."

"Clue me in," she urged. "If I'm going to love him, I have to know who he really is."

"I don't know how much you've heard, but when Joe was a kid, he and his old man had problems. Nothing major. Just father and son stuff. When Joe was eighteen, things came to a head the day before Thanksgiving. They got into an argument. Big Joe wanted Joe to spend the holiday deer hunting with him, but his mother wanted them home for a family dinner. Big Joe got his way, and he and Joe left for the deer camp.

"They kept at it once they arrived. They both said things they shouldn't have. When Big Joe went out in the field, Joe refused to go with him and stayed in camp. Later when he heard the rifle shot, he assumed Big Joe had bagged a buck. When it got late, and his dad didn't return, Joe went looking for him. He discovered the body hung up in a section of barbed wire. His father's rifle had discharged as he crawled through the fence."

"I had no idea." All she'd ever heard was that Big Joe

Mitchum had died in a hunting accident. As someone who deeply loved her own father, Mallory could well imagine Joe's horror. As a doctor, she knew the harsh effects such a trauma could have on the human psyche, especially that of a boy on the threshold of adulthood.

Briny went on. "Joe said he knew his father was dead. He tried to carry the body back to the truck. He couldn't manage. There was a reason they called him Big Joe. Joe had to leave him on the ground and drive ten miles for help, blaming himself all the way for what happened."

"But it wasn't his fault."

"Grief is as irrational as love, Mal. Joe believed if he hadn't angered his dad, if he'd gone out with him that day, even if he'd just been there to hold the fence, maybe he wouldn't have died."

"Did Joe receive counseling?" She hated to think he'd suffered through the pain and horror alone.

"I doubt it. Folks in Slapdown aren't real big on sharing their troubles. They prefer to tough it out, as you well know from your practice. I didn't meet Joe until a year later when I moved to town."

"You've known him a long time." She was grateful to Briny for giving her a glimpse of a side of him she hadn't known. Understanding a turning point in his life did not answer all the questions, but it helped her appreciate the tragic forces that had shaped his self-destructive behavior.

"Joe and I hit it off because we were both troubled, fatherless kids. We were alone in the world, so we counted on each other. Despite his problems and the messes he's made in other areas of his life, Joe's always been a good friend to me."

"The guilt explains why he dropped out of school," she observed.

"He said he tried to keep up but couldn't concentrate. All he could think about was the way his dad died, how he looked when Joe found him. I'm no shrink, but I think he plunged into a depression he couldn't shake off."

"You're probably right." Mallory berated herself. "Why didn't I see the obvious? I'm a doctor. I should have realized an intelligent kid from a good family doesn't become a lazy bum for no reason.''

"Joe was good at hiding from himself and from everyone else,'' Briny reminded her.

As a sixteen-year-old focused on her own future, she hadn't considered the far-reaching effects of Big Joe Mitchum's death on his son. She'd been away for ten hectic years, first to college, then to medical school and finally to San Antonio for her residency. When she'd returned to Slapdown after being gone so long, Joe was…just Joe. An aggravating ne'er-do-well who seemed determined to provoke her every chance he got.

"He gave up on himself, didn't he?'' She swallowed the lump in her throat. "He quit caring.''

Briny nodded. "I thought he might straighten up when he married Brandy. The poor kid tried but couldn't seem to help him get past the pain. They divorced not long after Chloe came along.''

"Do you honestly think being struck by lightning accomplished what no one else could?'' The answer to the mystery couldn't possibly be so simple.

"I don't know. Maybe. I noticed how different he was the day we went to Lubbock to buy the mobile home. Want to hear my theory?''

"Sure.''

"The lightning strike woke him up to life, but it was loving you that made him want to live it.''

You're the reason I'm here. He'd said those words more than once, but she'd never realized their significance. As early as she could remember, becoming a doctor had been *her* reason for living. Had the drive to heal been the inevitable force that had pushed her toward one crucial moment in time, insuring she would be there that stormy day with the knowledge to make Joe's heart beat again?

Was *he* the reason she was here?

Briny reached out and took her hand in both of his. "What is it, Mallory? You look like you just discovered a cure for the common cold.''

Hope and fear stole her breath. "Are Joe Mitchum and I

really meant to be together?'' she whispered. Was that what her life was all about? Loving Joe?

"Only you can say." Briny squeezed her hand. "All I know is he loves you. Except for myself, I've never seen a man so blind-eyed crazy about a woman. It's like he recognized who you were a long time ago."

"Who I am?"

"The one he's been waiting for," he said gently.

Mallory wiped her tears. "I know he's changed, but I'm afraid he hasn't changed enough." She told Briny about Glorieta. She hadn't known what her friend's reaction would be, but one thing she had not expected was laughter.

"I'm sorry." He wiped the grin off his face. "Is that what's put you into such a tailspin? You think Joe hooked up with that Tadlock woman again?"

"I don't *think* it. People saw them together. He came home the night of the GED smelling like cheap perfume and beer."

"Mallory, honey, Joe has been fending off Glorieta since he got out of the hospital. He was doing a pretty good job of it too, until that night." Briny calmly told her how an intoxicated Glorieta had accosted Joe in the parking lot. "He didn't trust her to drive, so he took her home."

"That wouldn't take three hours," she pointed out.

"She gave him the wrong directions. They ended way out in the country at the old Winslow place."

"That doesn't make sense. He knows where she lives."

"Apparently not. Anyway, she grabbed the keys out of the ignition and tossed them out the window. Joe said he spent over an hour looking for them."

"So why did he smell like beer?"

"Glorieta kept trying to get something started. When he told her no, she threw a beer at him. Fortunately, he ducked, but it splashed on his shirt."

"How do you know all this?" Tentative relief lightened the bitter burden of distrust. It would be such a relief to finally lay it down for good.

"He told me. I had to go to Slapdown on business a while

back, and I ran into Joe and Chloe when I stopped for lunch at the diner. He didn't mention seeing me?''

''No. I haven't exactly been on close speaking terms with him lately.''

''Look, Mal, Joe may have played around before, but that part of his life is behind him now. I can't answer all your questions, but I give you my word. You don't have to worry about other women. He worships the ground you walk on.'' Briny grinned. ''If I didn't know exactly how he felt, I'd think he was the one who was crazy.''

''You mean that?''

He nodded. ''He told me you're the only one for him, and I believe him. Regardless of what else he's done, Joe has never lied to me.''

Mallory held Briny's words close to her heart. Like a warm coat on a cold day, they began to chase away the icy chill of doubt. Not all of her questions had been answered. It was possible they never would be. Maybe Joe was right.

That was the way it had to be. Because some questions simply didn't have answers.

It was up to her now. All she had to do was let go of the rope of reason and walk off the ledge one step at a time, knowing there was no net to catch her. No guarantee. She would have to take a chance in order to receive one.

For once in her life, Mallory would accept that which could not be explained.

The house was too quiet without Chloe. She'd only been gone twenty-four hours, and already Joe missed her. He was her daddy now. What would she think when the old Joe came back? How would she handle another betrayal? Dammit! He didn't want to go.

The dog scratched at the door. Joe opened it and stepped outside, surprised when he saw how the day had changed. Despite a forecast of continued fair weather, the late afternoon sky was far too dark. The air was too cool for late July and carried the warning scent of rain. Wind shook the leaves in the cottonwoods and churned up tiny dust devils in the driveway. Rolling green-black clouds had gathered as quickly as an angry mob, blocking out the sun, and blanketing the landscape with an eerie yellow light. Far to the west, soundless lightning branded the horizon.

Lightning. A storm was coming.

Ordinary fickle weather? Or a sign that the guys in the Department of Natural Forces weren't very creative after all?

This was it. His frantic gaze shot up the hill. Mallory still wasn't home, and he dreaded to think of her driving in the storm. She'd been so hurt and angry when she'd left yesterday. He'd made a botch of things. He never should have pushed her. She wasn't ready to make the declarations of love that would save him. It was still too soon for her.

Even if time was running out for him.

He looked around. This was his home, but at any moment, he might have to leave it behind. Leave everything he'd worked for. He'd planned to visit with the retiring sheriff this afternoon about getting his election campaign off the ground. Who better to point him in the right direction than the man who'd held the office for the last sixteen years?

But what was the point? According to Celestian, he could be recalled any day. Any minute, from the looks of those storm clouds. The other Joe must be impatient to trade places. Would his replacement be interested in law enforcement? Would he rim-wreck everything he'd become by tearing down what had been so hard to build? Rage and frustration churned in his gut.

The promise of a new life didn't make losing this one any less painful. All memories of Will Pendleton would be wiped out, along with everything he'd experienced as Joe Mitchum. Any mistakes he made next time would be his own, not another man's. He'd be reborn. Start over with a clean slate.

He would lose any chance of spending eternity with Mallory.

He'd just been handed his death sentence. The last moments of his life were ticking away with every painful beat of his heart. Unlike a prisoner, he did not have the luxury of knowing when the end would come. But gut deep, he knew it would be soon. Too soon.

Unable to bear the silence that mocked him, he put the dog back in the house and drove to town. The wind picked up, and the sky grew darker by the minute. Not wanting to be alone, Joe headed for the diner.

Even a man on death row deserved a last meal.

"Hey, Joe!" Several people tore their gazes from the television behind the counter. It was tuned to a college football game, but severe weather updates scrolled across the bottom of the screen.

He acknowledged their greetings and climbed on a stool at the counter. Without looking at a menu, he ordered the Sunday special.

Dot filled his coffee cup. "Is it getting bad out there?"

"It got a lot worse between my place and here. The wind has really picked up." He sipped the coffee in an effort to calm the storm brewing inside him.

"They issued a severe storm warning. The TV weatherman said he'd never seen anything blow in so quick or come out of nowhere like this. They're saying it could turn into a tornado."

"A tornado, huh?" Maybe the fellas in Natural Forces were more creative than he thought.

Dot's face creased with worried wrinkles. "Strange how it churned up so sudden, isn't it?"

"Yeah." Joe's heart thumped in his chest. This was it. He ate the chicken fried steak dinner Dot served, but didn't taste it. He couldn't bear the thought of leaving without seeing Mallory again, or at least hearing the sound of her voice. He slipped off the stool and went to the pay phone. It rang several times before the machine clicked on and told him to leave a message. He hung up.

What could he say? He'd had his chance yesterday, and he'd let it slip through his fingers. He hadn't known they would send for him so soon. Why had he been allowed to resurrect Joe's life, only to forfeit it on a technicality?

When he returned to the counter, the other customers had

cleared out. Dot told him the severe storm warning had been upgraded to a tornado watch.

"You need to take shelter at the community center," he told her.

"I'll head over there when the tornado watch becomes a warning." She went about her business, bussing dishes and wiping tables. "You're welcome to stay here as long as you want, Joe."

"Thanks."

Half an hour later, the bell over the door jangled, and Sheriff Nate Egan blew in with a stiff gust of wind. He slapped rain off his hat. "I heard you were here, Joe. Since you're probably gonna be taking my place after the election, can you give me a hand?"

He wouldn't be here after the election. He might not even be here tomorrow. "Sure thing, Sheriff. What can I do?"

"Since we don't have any kind of siren system, I need you to help me notify folks there might be a tornado headed this way."

"Just tell me where you want me to go."

"Damn! Yesterday they were predicting clear skies and unseasonable heat. Where did this danged storm come from anyhow?"

Joe swallowed past the tightness in his throat. The Department of Natural Forces. Things were out of his hands now. He might as well do what little bit of good he could before his number was up.

Joe drove through the lashing rain to alert the residents in outlying areas. Many were old folks who needed serious convincing to leave their dry homes and head for the public storm shelter. As skittish as a new colt, Joe jumped every time a bolt of lightning speared down from the heavens. The thunder's cannon fire set his raw nerves on edge. Driving back to town in the blinding rain, he nearly ran off the road when a hot flash of light split a tree in half twenty yards away.

That was close.

His last stop was the tavern. When he pulled up in front of

Whiskey Pete's, there were only three cars in the parking lot, one of them Glorieta Tadlock's Chevy. He ran inside to make his appeal. The other customers dashed for their cars, but the sullen blonde refused to budge.

"I'm not going anywhere. It's raining hard enough to drown frogs." She turned back to the beer she was nursing.

"That's not all it's doing," Joe told her. "A tornado may be on the way. You need to get over to the community center as quick as you can."

She spun around on the barstool. "I don't have to do anything you say, Joe Mitchum. Who do you think you are, coming in here bossing people around? You're not the sheriff yet, you know."

"I'm just trying to insure the public safety."

"Don't worry about me. I'm a big girl."

Joe was tempted to lift her off the barstool and carry her to the shelter, but he couldn't spare the time. He had to call and find out if Mallory had made it home safely. Then he had to find the sheriff and see if there was anything else he could do. "Suit yourself, ma'am. But if you wait too long, you may be sorry."

Where had all this rain come from? When Mallory had left Fort Worth, the sun was shining and there hadn't been a cloud in the sky. The weather had remained clear most of the way home until just outside Slapdown when it suddenly turned dark and dangerous.

She had to drive slowly now because the downpour was so heavy she could only see a few feet of the road in front of her. Every few minutes, jagged forks of lightning lit up the world, followed by thunderclaps that rocked her little truck as it struggled through the deluge. The radio meteorologist had upgraded the tornado watch to a tornado warning when several funnel clouds were spotted in the area.

Despite the fury that raged around her, or maybe because of it, Mallory couldn't stop thinking about Joe. "That was the way it had to be" had taken on new significance since her talk with Briny. She was consumed by a powerful need to see

Joe. Hold him. Admit to him the love she'd finally admitted to herself. She had to find him. Today. A primal instinct deep inside urged her on. There was no time to lose. She couldn't wait until tomorrow.

Tomorrow would be too late.

She had no idea where the ominous warning came from, or what it meant. But between Fort Worth and Slapdown she'd come to a startling conclusion. Joe was not Joe. He was the mystery man from her vision. She hadn't realized it before because it was so impossibly illogical. Still, the signs were there. Roses and rings. Memories of another place and time. She might not know his name, but she knew *him*. She had seen him, achingly familiar, in Joe's dark eyes.

Another warning arrowed through her.

The man she loved was about to be lost to her.

She peered through the windshield into the violent blur of rain and cursed. If she didn't concentrate on her driving, she'd end up in a ditch. She couldn't let that happen. She had to get to Slapdown. To him.

As she drove, the swishing wiper blades hissed rhythmically in her ear. Hurry, hurry, hurry.

Mallory released a shaky sigh of relief when she finally pulled into town. The streets were deserted. She headed for the shelter at the community center, hoping to find Joe. He wouldn't try to sit out a tornado in his mobile home. He had to know how dangerous that could be. She spotted his truck when she turned the corner near The Bag and Wag. He stood outside the small grocery store helping owner Ben Smith nail a piece of plywood over a plate glass window shattered by a fallen tree. It was so large the leafy branches blocked the entry to the parking lot. She braked on the street and jumped out.

Within moments, the heavy rain soaked her to the skin, plastering her clothes to her body. A paralyzing premonition stopped her dead in her tracks. Goose bumps prickled along her skin, and she shivered. She looked up at the angry sky, and foreboding crawled up her spine. A blinding bolt of lightning pierced the clouds and struck a utility pole at the side of the store. The wind-tossed scene dissolved into slow motion as she watched a downed electrical line fly from the pole. It seemed to take on a life of its own as it twisted and whipped in the wind. Shooting sparks like a fire-breathing serpent, it lashed down toward the store.

Ben Smith had stepped inside, but Joe stood squarely in the path of the killer cable. No. This could not be happening again. Instead of panic, an unearthly calm washed over Mallory. She stilled, listening as the quiet voice of her heart told her what to do.

Cupping her hands to her mouth, she screamed above the howling wind. "I love you, Joe. I have always loved you. I want to stay with you forever."

In response to her shouted declaration, Joe wheeled around. Missing him by inches, the live wire fell harmlessly to the ground as though a switch had been thrown, cutting off its deadly power. The unremitting wind stopped with uncanny abruptness. Overhead, dark clouds scattered as though parted by an unseen hand. The sun, brighter than Mallory ever remembered it, shone down on her as she rushed into Joe's arms.

"I love you, too." He held Mallory close, and she clung to him in a desperate, joyful embrace. When his lips found hers, it was Joe who saw a vision. A vision of the life they would share. The memories of Will Pendleton gently faded from his mind until all that were left were the ones he'd made with Mallory. She had completed him and made him whole.

"You're him, aren't you?" Incredulous tears streamed from her eyes and mingled with raindrops.

He cupped her face in his hands. "Of course I'm him. I'm the real Joe Mitchum. The man who's going to make you happy for the rest of your life."

"And even after that?"

Gazing deeply into Mallory's eyes he saw the future shimmering in their golden depths. She knew the truth, and so did he. They would have more than one lifetime together.

They would have eternity.

Epilogue

The mysterious storm raged around Glorieta Tadlock as she hightailed it out of Whiskey Pete's and slid behind the wheel of her pea-green Chevette. If Pete hadn't decided to close early, she wouldn't have to drive in this mess.

She sure wasn't leaving on Joe Mitchum's orders. Nobody told her what to do, especially him. He wasn't the law yet, even if everybody in town said he would be soon enough. She gunned the motor and pointed the little car down the road, ducking her head to peer through the windshield at a sky filled with thrashing black clouds. The farther she went the more convinced she was that a tornado might really be on the way.

Dang! She'd automatically started for home when she should have headed back to town and the storm shelter. Too late now. She'd passed the point of no return. It would take just as long to turn around and drive back as it would to get to her house. She didn't have a cellar, but she had a bathtub and a mattress. That's all she needed. Steering with one knee, her hands shook as she unwrapped several sticks of Juicy Fruit and crammed the fragrant gum into her mouth.

Just ahead, a funnel cloud snaked down from the boiling sky like the devil's own bullwhip. Before Glorieta could react and grab the steering wheel, the cyclone swooped up the Chevette and pulled it into the swirling darkness. Horrified by the screaming wind and flying debris that enveloped her, she choked on the large wad of gum that had been meant to calm her nerves.

In the quiet white vastness of the After Place, Celestian passed through the endless corridors pushing a cart laden with sorted prayers. It was now his job to deliver the missives to the appropriate saints and angels. Might as well work with Sam the janitor, for all the chance he had of getting his old job back. It would take centuries of good conduct to remove the demerits from his record.

Hearing a commotion as he passed the time-out room, he stopped and peeked inside. What a surprise. The instigator of the disturbance was none other than the old Joe Mitchum reacting to the cancellation of his return flight by throwing a tantrum that would have made Bonaparte look like a novice. The rookie monitor was the assertive sort, barking back as the angry spirit berated him. It wouldn't be long before he reached the end of his astral rope.

Celestian could certainly sympathize. However, dealing with annoying spirits who had been timed-out because they were deemed Unfit for Return was no longer his problem. He was the prayer courier now. He pushed the heavy cart past the doorway, glancing in idly at the spirit monitor. Suddenly he stopped, backed up. Looked again. A wicked smile creased his face as inspiration battled temptation. No. He shouldn't. Taking matters into his own hands was the root of all his troubles.

Still, things had turned out all right for Mallory Peterson and her real Joe. What was the harm of giving the new time-out monitor the benefit of his experience? One little suggestion. The more he thought about it, the more it seemed like his responsibility to point out the obvious.

If the old Joe's angry spirit wanted to go back to Slapdown, fine.

There just happened to be a vacancy.

* * *

The storm abated as suddenly and inexplicably as it had started. When the wind stopped, the Chevette fell from the sky like a rock and plunked down in an open field. The impact dislodged the wad of chewing gum that had blocked Glorieta Tadlock's airway, and her recently vacated mortal coil drew a gasping breath.

The coil's new resident looked around in confusion, but panic didn't set in until she glanced down and spotted the ring piercing her bellybutton. The butterfly tattoo on her shoulder.

No. It can't be! Somebody tell me this is not happening.

As the real Joe could have told the old Joe, waking up in a strange body would be a whole new experience.

* * * * *

It's romantic comedy with a kick
(in a pair of strappy pink heels)!

Introducing

HARLEQUIN®
flipside™

"It's chick-lit with the romance and happily-ever-after ending that Harlequin is known for."
—*USA TODAY* bestselling author Millie Criswell, author of *Staying Single*, October 2003

"Even though our heroine may take a few false steps while finding her way, she does it with wit and humor."
—Dorien Kelly, author of *Do-Over*, November 2003

Launching October 2003.
Make sure you pick one up!

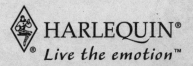

HARLEQUIN®
Live the emotion™

Visit us at www.harlequinflipside.com

HFGENERIC

✂ **Your opinion is important to us!** Please take a few moments to share your
thoughts with us about your experiences with Harlequin and Silhouette books.
Your comments will be very useful in ensuring that we deliver books you love to read.
*Please take a few minutes to complete the questionnaire,
then send it to us at the address below.*

Send your completed questionnaires to:
Harlequin/Silhouette Reader Survey, P.O. Box 9046, Buffalo, NY 14269-9046

---

1. As you may know, there are many different lines under the Harlequin and Silhouette
   brands. Each of the lines is listed below. Please check the box that most represents
   your reading habit for each line.

Line	Currently read this line	Do not read this line	Not sure if I read this line
Harlequin American Romance	❑	❑	❑
Harlequin Duets	❑	❑	❑
Harlequin Romance	❑	❑	❑
Harlequin Historicals	❑	❑	❑
Harlequin Superromance	❑	❑	❑
Harlequin Intrigue	❑	❑	❑
Harlequin Presents	❑	❑	❑
Harlequin Temptation	❑	❑	❑
Harlequin Blaze	❑	❑	❑
Silhouette Special Edition	❑	❑	❑
Silhouette Romance	❑	❑	❑
Silhouette Intimate Moments	❑	❑	❑
Silhouette Desire	❑	❑	❑

2. Which of the following best describes why you bought *this book?* One answer only,
   please.

the picture on the cover	❑	the title ❑
the author	❑	the line is one I read often ❑
part of a miniseries	❑	saw an ad in another book ❑
saw an ad in a magazine/newsletter	❑	a friend told me about it ❑
I borrowed/was given this book	❑	other: _____ ❑

3. Where did you buy *this book?* One answer only, please.

at Barnes & Noble	❑	at a grocery store ❑
at Waldenbooks	❑	at a drugstore ❑
at Borders	❑	on eHarlequin.com Web site ❑
at another bookstore	❑	from another Web site ❑
at Wal-Mart	❑	Harlequin/Silhouette Reader ❑
at Target	❑	Service/through the mail
at Kmart	❑	used books from anywhere ❑
at another department store		I borrowed/was given this ❑
or mass merchandiser		book

4. On average, how many Harlequin and Silhouette books do you buy at one time?

   I buy _____ books at one time ❑
   I rarely buy a book ❑

MRQ403SR-1A

5. How many times per month do you shop for any *Harlequin and/or Silhouette* books? One answer only, please.

    1 or more times a week ❑   a few times per year ❑
    1 to 3 times per month ❑   less often than once a year ❑
    1 to 2 times every 3 months ❑   never ❑

6. When you think of your ideal heroine, which *one* statement describes her the best? One answer only, please.

    She's a woman who is strong-willed ❑   She's a desirable woman ❑
    She's a woman who is needed by others ❑   She's a powerful woman ❑
    She's a woman who is taken care of ❑   She's a passionate woman ❑
    She's an adventurous woman ❑   She's a sensitive woman ❑

7. The following statements describe types or genres of books that you may be interested in reading. Pick *up to 2 types* of books that you are most interested in.

    I like to read about truly romantic relationships ❑
    I like to read stories that are sexy romances ❑
    I like to read romantic comedies ❑
    I like to read a romantic mystery/suspense ❑
    I like to read about romantic adventures ❑
    I like to read romance stories that involve family ❑
    I like to read about a romance in times or places that I have never seen ❑
    Other: _____ ❑

The following questions help us to group your answers with those readers who are similar to you. Your answers will remain confidential.

8. Please record your year of birth below.
    19 ____

9. What is your marital status?
    single ❑   married ❑   common-law ❑   widowed ❑
    divorced/separated ❑

10. Do you have children 18 years of age or younger currently living at home?
    yes ❑   no ❑

11. Which of the following best describes your employment status?
    employed full-time or part-time ❑   homemaker ❑   student ❑
    retired ❑   unemployed ❑

12. Do you have access to the Internet from either home or work?
    yes ❑   no ❑

13. Have you ever visited eHarlequin.com?
    yes ❑   no ❑

14. What state do you live in?
    _____

15. Are you a member of Harlequin/Silhouette Reader Service?
    yes ❑   Account # _____   no ❑   MRQ403SR-1B

SILHOUETTE *Romance*®

COMING NEXT MONTH

#1690 HER PREGNANT AGENDA—Linda Goodnight
Marrying the Boss's Daughter

General Counsel Grant Lawson agreed to protect Ariana Fitzpatrick—and her unborn twins—from her custody-seeking, two-timing ex-fiancé. But delivering the precious babies and kissing their oh-so-beautiful mother senseless weren't in his job description! And falling in love—well, that *definitely* wasn't part of the agenda!

#1691 THE VISCOUNT & THE VIRGIN—Valerie Parv
The Carramer Trust

Legend claimed anyone who served the Merrisand Trust would find true love, but the only thing Rowe Sevrin, Viscount Aragon, found was feisty, fiery-haired temptress Kirsten Bond. How could his reluctant assistant seem so innocent and inexperienced and still be a mother? And why was her young son Rowe's spitting image?

#1692 THE MOST ELIGIBLE DOCTOR
—Karen Rose Smith

Nurse Brianne Barrington had lost every person she'd ever loved. So when she took the job with Jed Sawyer, a rugged, capable doctor with emotional wounds of his own, she intended to keep her distance. But Jed's tender embraces awakened a womanly desire she'd never felt before. Could the cautious, love-wary Brianna risk her heart again?

#1693 MARLIE'S MYSTERY MAN—Doris Rangel
Soulmates

Marlie Simms was falling for two men—sort of! One man was romantic, sexy and funny, and the other was passionate, determined and strong. Except they were *both* Caid Matthews—a man whose car accident left his spirit split in two! And only Marlie's love could make Caid a whole man again....